FOREVER PRINCETON CHARMING

C.M. SEABROOK

FRANKIE LOVE

Copyright © 2019 by C.M. Seabrook, Frankie Love

All rights reserved.

No part of this book may be reproduced in any form or by any electronic or mechanical means, including information storage and retrieval systems, without written permission from the author, except for the use of brief quotations in a book review.

FOREVER PRINCETON CHARMING

He's fighting for their fairy tale.

Charlotte Hayes lost her slipper – err shoe – the first night she met Spencer Beckett, A.K.A. Princeton Charming. She fell into his arms and their lives were changed. *Forever*.

> *One kiss and she was smitten.*
> *One date and she was head over heels.*
> *One tragedy and her heart was his.*

They may want the same thing, but someone is determined to take what they've fought so hard for – and now Charlie is fighting for her life.

If Spencer loses the woman he loves ... they'll never get their happily-ever-after.

Will they get the fairy tale ending they both deserve?

** Forever Princeton Charming is the final book in the four-book Princeton Charming series.

1

SPENCER

I'M LOSING HER. This can't be happening.

I pace the sterile hallway as doctors and nurses yell and scramble in the small ICU room, trying to restart Charlie's heart. But all I can hear is the monotonous beep of the monitor.

Flatline.

And it's like my own heart has stopped. It may as well have. Because I don't think I'll survive if she doesn't.

"Come on, Charlie. Fight. Don't do this." I tug at my hair, tears burning my eyes and blurring my vision. I've experienced loss, but this...this feeling, like some essential part of me has cracked in half, it's unbearable. "Please, God. Don't take her from me."

Tatum is behind me, his own anguish and fear palpable. I struggle to hold myself back from beating the last breath from his lungs for his part in this. But there's still a twisted feeling inside me that wonders if Charlie was wrong about his involvement.

But I can't care about that right now, not while she's fighting for her life, while there's still a chance she can come back to me.

"Come on, Charlie," I demand through gritted teeth, like my own desire for her to live can somehow restart her heart. "Please."

And then the monotonous beep stops. There's a second of silence. A second that seems like a goddamn eternity. A second when I fear the worst, that the medical team has given up. And then I hear it.

Beep.

Beep.

Beep.

A steady, but slow sound that signals a pulse, and a sob rips from my chest.

The doctor continues to bark orders and the next thing I know they're wheeling the gurney through the door and down the hall. I'm pushed back and I only get a small glimpse of Charlie's pale face before they're rushing her away.

I grab one of the nurse's arms and ask, "Where are they taking her?"

She frowns down at my hand and I release her. "The OR," she says, gaze softening. "Can you find your way back to the family waiting room? Someone will come in and talk to you when we know more."

I want to argue with her, demand to know more now, insist that she tell me Charlie's going to be okay. But I know that I'm just holding her back from doing her job - saving my girlfriend's life.

"Yeah. I can find my way back." I give a hard nod, and she turns and follows after Charlie.

I drag my hands over my face and take in a few steadying breaths, feeling like my legs might just give out on me any second.

Across from me, Tatum gives me a wary look. He's leaning against the wall, face almost as white as Charlie's had been, and he looks as miserable as I feel.

I can't do this here. Because I swear to god, if the guy says one word, I'll have him laid out on the hospital floor. So I walk away, toward the small, private room where Jill and Daphne are waiting.

They stand when I walk in.

"How is she?" Jill asks, and I realize they have no clue what just happened, that we almost lost her.

That we may still lose her.

I sink down into one of the chairs and bury my head in my hands, feeling nauseous. I'm not sure where the hell Prescott has disappeared to, but I could use him here now.

"Spencer?" Jill sits beside me. "You're scaring me. Tell me how Charlie is."

"They just took her into the OR," Tatum says from the door, voice broken. "Her heart stopped—"

"Someone needs to get that bastard out of here, before I kill him," I growl out, standing, but Jill stands with me, placing herself between us. She equals my height, but I could easily push past her to wrap my hands around Tatum's throat.

"You want to tell me why you think I have anything to do with this?" Tatum spits out, a flash of anger in his hard gaze.

"Charlie saw you. You ran her off the fucking road, then left her there to die."

His eyes widen. "Jesus, Beckett, you're delusional."

"I don't know why you think Tatum would do that." Jill is frowning at me, hand on my chest stopping me from going after him. "He was with me all night. We were studying at the library when I got your call."

My right eye twitches and I look between them, not sure what to believe. Why the hell would Charlie make it up? She wouldn't.

Daphne has remained silent the entire time, but she pipes up now, "I don't get it. Charlie said she saw Tatum?"

I rub the back of my neck and go through the conversation. "She said it was a Taurus that had been following her."

"Right." Tatum blows out an exasperated breath. "And I'm the only fucking guy in Princeton who drives one, so of course it had to be me."

"She saw you get out of the car." I scrub my hands over my face, a tickling at the back of my neck knowing something isn't right, but needing someone to blame, to lash out at. "After the accident. She saw your sweatshirt, the one..." What had she said? "The one with the bleach stain."

Tatum shakes his head and unzips his coat, then takes it off. He's wearing a Princeton hoodie, but there isn't a stain on it. "I lost that fucking sweatshirt months ago." He looks bewildered, and hurt when he asks, "Charlie believes I tried to hurt her?"

"We all know Tatum would never..." Jill starts, but I give her a hard look, because right now, I'm not sure of anything...or anyone.

"Fuck," I mutter, pinching my fingers at the bridge of my nose.

I place my hands on the back of my head and pace, then sit down again. Any adrenaline that I had before is now gone, and I feel drained, numb. None of this makes sense, but I also realize that Tatum being involved in any of this makes the least sense.

Tense silence fills the room, and both Jill and Daphne sit back down. Tatum still hovers in the doorway, looking like a wounded dog. And I get it. If I was a better person, I might care that his feelings are hurt, but right now I only have enough in me to worry about Charlie.

Seconds, minutes, hours, tick by, and no one says anything as we wait. Prescott keeps texting me. Thinking Charlie was okay, he'd gone back to check on Ava, who's still shaken up about her dorm room being doused in pig's blood. I told him to keep her at his place, even though they both insisted they come back. But there's nothing they can do here.

Nothing any of us can do but wait and pray.

And I do. I'm not a religious person, but I beg whatever God will listen to save her.

But the longer we wait, the more time that passes, hope leaves me. And I can see it fading in Tatum as well. He's sitting on the floor now, on the opposite side of the room, and when I glance over at him, he looks away.

"Say something to him," Jill says so that only I can hear.

But what the fuck am I supposed to say? Sorry that I thought you tried to kill your best friend? Sorry that I punched you in the face without giving you the benefit of the doubt. Either of those would do, but I just close my eyes and shake my head.

"I'm going to get some snacks, see if the cafeteria is still open," Daphne says. How she can think of food at a time like this is beyond me.

"I'll go with you." Jill stands and follows her out, and I realize that maybe it isn't about being hungry. It's about needing something to do. The alternative is pacing the corridors with panic.

Alone with Tatum, I lean back in my chair and glance over at him. His eye is already changing colors from where I hit him, and it'll be completely black tomorrow.

"Sorry about the eye," I mutter.

He grunts and looks away, arms crossed over his chest. "You think I couldn't have taken you out with one shot if I wanted to?"

It's the second time I've hit him, and he's right, with his size and strength, I wouldn't have a chance if he ever fought back.

"Why didn't you?" I ask.

He holds my gaze for a moment, and I wonder if he's not thinking about taking a shot now. But then he shakes his head and mutters, "Because I knew you must have had a reason..." He stands, then sits down across from me where Daphne had been sitting before, burying his head in his hands. "I'd never hurt her, not on purpose. That she thought... shit... I'd rather die than—"

"Yeah. I believe you."

His head jerks up and he meets my gaze, there's a coldness in his eyes, a fierceness that I've never seen before. "You think I give a shit about what you believe? It's Charlotte who I..." He shakes his head and looks away. "What fucking reason would I have to hurt her?"

"Jealousy," I spit out, regretting it the second I say it. But it's what I'd been thinking originally. That he couldn't stand her being with me.

His lips turn up in a sneer. "You think I'm

jealous of you? I feel sorry for you. Because with all your money, all your influence, you'll never be the man she needs."

I let out a heavy sigh, and I know I deserve his words, his anger. "You might be right, but I'm willing to try every day of my life to become that man."

He grunts, his gaze unfocused when he looks away. "You'll fail."

"Maybe." But I'm not going to be a coward ever again, letting her go because I think she deserves better. She does. But if she survives this, I'll do everything in my power to be the better she deserves.

More silence. More seconds. More minutes. They stretch, like a never-ending void until a woman in scrubs comes into the room.

Both Tatum and I stand in unison, but neither of us are brave enough to ask the dreaded question.

"Charlotte is in recovery," she says, her expression unreadable.

Tatum and I let out a collective sigh and he sits back down, muttering, "Thank god."

"So she's going to be all right?" I ask.

"She's stable. There was a small clot that moved to her heart." The woman keeps talking, medical terms and treatments that are way over my head. But I heard the only thing that matters - Charlie is alive.

"Can I see her?" I need to see her. Need to hold her hand. See her chest rise and fall with each breath.

"I'll have someone come for you when she's able to have visitors."

I want to argue with her, to demand to be taken to Charlie, but I know it would be useless.

When the doctor leaves I sink back into my chair. "She's okay." The words are for me, and I have to repeat it a few times. "She's going to be all right."

Tears burn my eyes and when I glance over at Tatum, he's dragging his fingers over his own, wiping the tears away.

My phone beeps and I see a message from Daniel, Charlie's dad. He's landed at the airport and is on his way to the hospital. I exhale, grateful that one thing went according to plan. Getting Daniel here, to be at Charlie's side was important, but I'm still surprised at the tears that I can't blink away.

I can barely get the news out when Jill and Daphne return. Thankfully, Tatum seems to be more articulate than I am, reciting verbatim what the doctor said.

"I knew she'd be all right," Daphne says, hugging Tatum. "There's no one tougher than Charlotte."

"You okay?" Jill asks, sitting down in the plastic hospital chair beside me and offering me a Twizzler.

"Okay?" I shake my head, my stomach churning at the thought of food. "I don't think I'll ever be okay again."

Jill places her hand on my arm. "You really love her, don't you?"

"So damn much. The thought of losing her..." I choke on the words as I see Charlie's pale face, hear the flatline in my mind. I rub my eyes, feeling broken, like at any second my world will turn upside down again.

"She's in recovery, she's going to be okay," Jill says with authority. "You have to believe that. For Charlie." She gives me a small smile. "You know positive energy and all that."

"You always so cool and collected?" I ask, not feeling the confidence she speaks with.

"I want to be a campaign manager, so I've spent a lot of time practicing how to deal with stress."

She shrugs. "Also, I grew up with a mother who relied on me for a lot of things. It made me grow up fast. But what I do know is that Daphne is right, Charlie's a fighter. She'll get through this and be stronger for it." She squeezes my arm. "And we'll be there to help her."

I realize I needed Jill's positive words. And when Charlie wakes up, she'll need us all to be strong for her. Not the broken mess I am right now.

"She's lucky to have you for a friend," I say.

Jill gives a small smile. "I think we both know it's us who are lucky to have her."

"Yeah. I won't argue with that."

A few minutes later, Ava and Prescott enter the room carrying a paper tray of coffees. I told them to wait until Charlie woke up to come back, but my chest tightens when I see them. I'm glad they didn't listen to me, because I need them now, more than ever.

Jill smiles as Ava hands her a cup. "Thank you. I need this, we've been up all night."

"We figured," Ava says as I stand pulling my little sister into a hug. "You hanging in there?" she asks. Her eyes are filled with worry that matches my own.

"Barely." Memories of the night we lost Ethan

surface, and it's painful, being here in a hospital again. That I almost lost Charlie the same way I lost my brother. "I'll be better once I can see her."

Ava hugs me harder before releasing me, and I know she's been through her own hell tonight.

"Anything back from campus security or the police on the vandalism?" I ask, taking the coffee from Prescott.

Daphne and Tatum join us, everyone anxious for details. For any answer at all. A reason for this madness.

"The cops came, did a shit show job as far as I consider," Prescott says. "But the crime scene had already been compromised by the time Ava had gotten there. Her roommate had already shown up with half the lacrosse team." He shakes his head, then places an arm around my little sister, before adding through gritted teeth, "The police chalked it up to college pranks."

"Are you fucking kidding me?" Tatum spits out, fury in his eyes. "It's more than that. Hell, Charlie was run off the road." We're all on edge, but Tatum puts our frustration to words. "Can't the cops put two and two together? If they can't do their job, then maybe we—"

"You have questions for us, son?" a uniformed

officer asks from the doorway, another behind him. There's a challenge in the way the man looks at Tatum.

"Yeah, I want to know what you're doing to catch whoever did this." Tatum moves toward the cops and his jaw twitches, anger and tension vibrating off him.

I know his protective streak over Charlie could get him in trouble. And I get it. I want to fight the whole world right now, shit I already threw a punch at Tatum. And I can feel his need to come to blows with someone over it. But fighting the police will only get his ass thrown in jail.

Prescott seems to notice it too, and he steps in front of Tatum, giving him a look and saying something under his breath that seems to settle him slightly.

"Have you located the Taurus?" I ask the officer whose badge reads Delacorte. "The guy responsible?"

"That's what we're here for, to find out more information about what happened tonight." He's an older man with a gruff voice and his partner comes off much the same. As if they've been drinking black coffee for forty years, with tired eyes and weighted down shoulders. They don't exactly give me confidence.

Still, knowing they are the guys we got on the case, I explain the conversation I had with Charlie, telling them what she told me. The car, the hooded man, the sweatshirt with the stain. I don't mention Charlie's suspicion about it being Tatum, knowing deep down that there's no way he was involved.

Delacorte and his partner Mitchell dutifully take notes, but I don't have much faith that they are going to find the guy who tried to kill the woman I love.

If Charlie's stalker is going to be found, I have a feeling it's going to be because of me.

No one else loves her like I do. No one else needs to protect her the way I must.

The way I promised I would.

"We'll wait until she wakes up to get her story, but thanks, Spencer, for the information," Delacorte says.

"That's it?" Tatum growls out.

Delacorte gives him a hard look. "Without any witnesses and considering that the other car never hit Ms. Hayes', we're doing the best we can working off little information."

"And the dorm rooms?" Tatum isn't backing

down. "And the blog posts. The threats. You're really going to do nothing?"

"We're doing our job, son."

Tatum points a finger at him. "Well, you're doing a really shitty one."

Prescott pulls him back as I move to shake the officer's hand. "Thank you."

Delacorte takes my hand, his features tight. "We'll be in touch."

I nod, my heart racing as I look over at Tatum. He looks like a bull ready to fight. He loves Charlie, not the way I do, but he loves her all the same.

I've got to find the person who did this, and even though it kills me, I know Tatum is going to be the person to help.

2

CHARLIE

Trying to wake up is like digging through a thick fog that wraps around me, heavy and warm and somewhat comforting. Sounds are what come to me first. A machine beeping steadily, people talking in the distance. And then scent. Something harsh, chemical - I know the smell, it's familiar and reminds me of my mom.

I'm in the hospital.

Memories rush back. Someone following me. The car coming from nowhere. Me trying to swerve and miss it. The tree. Then pain.

And Tatum...

I groan, not wanting to believe it.

"Hey, kiddo," my dad's voice fills me, and when

I blink, his face is above mine, eyes filled with love and concern. "I'm here baby girl."

"Da-daddy," I choke out, my throat dry and scratchy, but so glad that he's here. But he's not the only person I need right now. "Where's..." I swallow, but it hurts to do so, and look around the sterile room. "Where's Spencer?"

"He's in the hall talking to the police again. Your friends are here too."

My friends?

"Your roommate Daphne, and Jill, and I met Spencer's sister Ava. I'm not sure about the boy she's with, but—"

"And Tatum?" I ask.

My dad nods. "He's here."

I don't know how to feel about that. I still don't know if what I saw was real. It doesn't make sense. Why would Tatum want to hurt me? But I know without any doubt that the man outside my car was wearing his sweatshirt. Because I'm the one who put the bleach stain there. I'd been so upset with myself for ruining it, knowing like me Tatum didn't have a lot of money. But he'd just laughed about it, and shrugged it off.

"Just makes it more authentic," Tatum had joked.

How could that same man be the one who tried to hurt me?

I try to shift in bed, but it hurts, and I'm bogged down with wires and tubes that seem to be everywhere.

"Careful, now," my dad says, helping me raise the bed so that I'm sitting up slightly.

"Wha-what happened?" I'd been fine. I was talking to Spencer, and then Tatum came in. They were arguing, and Spencer had hit him. I'd felt something tighten in my chest, a sharp pain, and I couldn't breathe...then everything went dark.

"You had a blood clot from one of your injuries. But you're going to be all right." My dad squeezes my hand and kisses my forehead. He looks tired, haunted, like he's trying to be strong, but barely holding on by a thread. He's already been through so much. I can't imagine what he must have felt when he got the call that I was in the hospital.

Emotions strangle me, and I choke out, "I'm sorry."

"For what?" He rests a hand on my forehead, stroking my hair back like he used to do when I was a little girl.

"For scaring you like this."

He sighs softly. "I'm just glad you're okay, and I

can be here. That boyfriend of yours...he really cares about you."

"I know." I smile, feeling some of the anxiety leave me.

The door opens and Spencer comes in. His dark blond hair sticks up at odd angles, and I know he's been tugging at it like he does when he's worried or stressed out.

"You're awake." Relief fills his eyes, and he moves to the opposite side of the bed from my dad and leans down, then presses a gentle kiss to my temple. Dark scruff coats his jaw, and there are bruises under his eyes. He looks like he's been through hell and back and I realize that my dad must have given me the sugar-coated version about what happened.

"Hey," I whisper, twining my fingers with his.

My dad clears his throat and stands. "I'm going to go get some dinner. I'll be back soon."

"Dinner?" I ask Spencer when my dad is gone. "How long have I been out?"

He sits beside me, and lifts my fingers to his lips, kissing my knuckles. There are tears in his eyes that I can tell he's trying to hold back.

"Spence?" I say when he doesn't speak.

"I... shit... I lost you, Charlie," he finally chokes out. "You left me."

I frown at him, not understanding.

"Your heart stopped, and I thought..." He takes in a breath and it's ragged, tortured. "You need to promise me you'll never leave me again. Can't...can't live without you, Charlie."

"I promise." I want to gather him in my arms, take away all the torment I see in his eyes, but I'm too weak, so I just squeeze his hand, and tell him, "I love you, Spencer."

He leans over and kisses me. His lips are soft, gentle, but there's something almost desperate in his touch, like he needs proof that I'm really here. I can tell he's holding back, can feel his anguish.

"I love you so much I think it might destroy me," he murmurs against my mouth, pressing his forehead to mine, his palm resting on my cheek.

We stay locked like that for a long moment.

Finally, he pulls back, and his voice is rough when he says, "There are police outside. They want to take your statement once you feel strong enough."

"Okay," I say, even though talking about what happened is the last thing I want to do right now.

Especially if it means having to tell them about Tatum. I don't think I can do that.

I blink back tears, confused and hurting.

"Hey. You're okay. I'm never going to let anything happen to you again. And we'll find who did this."

"Tatum," I whisper, feeling like I'm betraying him, just by saying his name.

"Yeah...there's something you should know." Spencer's brows form a deep V and he brushes my hair away from my cheek, his thumb stroking my jaw. "It wasn't Tatum, Charlie. He was with Jill all night. Whoever was wearing his sweatshirt, it wasn't him."

It wasn't him?

Of course it wasn't.

A mix of emotions floods me, the most poignant - guilt.

"Does he..." I lick my dry lips. "Does he know I thought it was him?"

Spencer winces and nods.

Oh god.

"He's still here. He wants to see you. But the cops need to speak with you first."

I close my eyes. "I don't want to replay it, Spence."

"I know, babe, but you need to. If we want to find who did this, we need to follow every lead. And telling them what happened might spark a memory."

I nod, a tear falling down my cheek, which Spencer wipes away. "Tell them to come in. Let's just get this over with."

Spencer leans over me, kissing me softly, and cupping my cheek with his hand. "I hate that you're here, hooked up to IVs. I wish you were home, in my bed."

His words cover me with a warmth I need. "I wish for that too. Soon."

"Not sure I'm ever going to let you leave it once I get you back there," he says, but it's not desire that fuels the comment, I can hear the possessiveness in his voice, the need to protect me. He walks away, looking at me before opening the door. "I love you, Charlie Hayes."

"I love you more, Spencer Beckett."

And I do. So much.

I thought I was gone. The light came for me and I thought it was over. I'd felt my mother's love, her soft hands and her big hugs...and for a moment I'd wanted to stay there. But then she brought me back. Carried me through, filling me with strength to fight. It sounds unbelievable, but I know it's the truth.

I'm alive.

Here.

Breathing.

And I will never, ever take it for granted.

When the officers, Delacorte and Mitchell, come in to speak with me, I recount the night before. Tearing up as I tell them about the aggressive driver, how he kept getting closer, and closer, how the car disappeared and then seemed to come out of nowhere and I had to swerve, sending me spinning across the black ice and into a tree.

By the time I finish explaining everything, I'm shaking and exhausted. I'm grateful when a nurse comes in and tells them I need to rest.

I wrap myself up in the flimsy hospital blanket as best I can, but I'm still cold. I want my own bed, my own things.

As if reading my mind, Tatum comes in with my favorite blanket tucked under an arm, the quilt my grandmother made for me.

"I know you aren't supposed to have visitors, but I knew you'd want this," he says, spreading the blanket out over me, avoiding making eye contact. "Somehow this escaped being ruined. It was actually Daphne's side of the room that took the brunt of the damage."

I'd forgotten about my dorm room being vandalized, and I'm glad that I didn't see what was done.

"Thank you, I was hoping someone would bring me this," I say, emotion washing over me. "You know me so well."

His shoulders tense and his hands still, but he recovers quickly. "I know you like to be cozy. Thought this would help."

"It does," I say, reaching for him. He flinches and tears streak my cheeks. "Look at me, Tatum."

He shakes his head, trembling.

"Look at me, please," I plead with him.

Finally he does. His eyes are glassy, his emotion on display. "I thought I was losing you all over again, Charlotte."

"You didn't. I'm right here."

He swallows, and I want to reach out and pull him to me. I want to breathe in his familiar smells and be reminded of home, where I come from, where I always thought I'd want to be. He's been my best friend since I came to Princeton, and I don't want to lose him. But he's pulling back even now, wiping his eyes and stepping away.

"Tatum—"

"No, Charlotte. That's just it. I *did* lose you. I thought...fuck...I love you." He takes in a ragged breath. "You know that, and yet..." There's so much pain in his eyes when he looks at me. "You thought...God, how could you really think that I'd hurt you?"

"I know," I say, tears spilling from my eyes. "I was wrong. But I was scared and in shock and I thought..." I shake my head, shame flooding me. "I'm so sorry Tatum."

He stands at the end of the bed, fingers curling around the steel frame and closes his eyes. "I didn't come in here to upset you."

"I just want us to be good. I'm so sorry."

He shakes his head. "You don't have to apologize. You believed what you saw, the Taurus, the sweater—" His mouth clamps down on the words and his nostrils flare, and there's a flash in his eyes, a spark like he remembered something. Then he pins me with a look that sends a shiver down my spine. "You said the guy was the same size as me?"

"I know it wasn't you. That you'd never hurt me."

His eyes go dark, and a vengeance covers him, in a way I've never seen before. "You're right, Charlie. I wouldn't hurt you, but I think I know who would."

Not even my grandmother's quilt can take away the cold that fills me.

"Who?" I ask, both scared and desperate to know who he thinks would be so hateful to spread pig's blood all over Ava's and my room, who would send a rock hurtling through my window, who would write blog posts and send threatening texts. Who would use Ethan's death as a tactic to scare me.

It worked.

I'm terrified.

I can't trust anyone but the people who are here with me now. My world is small, and that's fine by me. I don't want to let anyone in that might want to hurt me. Hurt the people I love.

"Tatum?" I ask again when I watch the tick in his jaw increase.

"Decan," Tatum finally says, his voice fueled by anger. He turns then, but not before I see the resolve in his eyes. He has a plan. One that will probably get him in trouble, or worse.

"Wait, Tatum, talk to the cops, they might—"

But he's already gone.

"What's with him?" Spencer asks as he comes

into the room, glancing over his shoulder where Tatum just disappeared.

"He thinks the person who did this might be Decan. You have to stop him from doing something stupid." I barely get the words out before Spencer is darting out of the room in the same direction as Tatum.

3

SPENCER

"You ready to do this?" Tatum asks me as we pull up to the three-story apartment complex where Decan lives.

I park the car and look up at the building, knowing we're about to break a dozen laws, if we follow Tatum's plan. But we've given the police two whole days, and they've done nothing.

"Can't risk him striking out at Charlie again," I say, opening my door.

The police have already questioned Decan, and from what they told me, he had a solid alibi for the night of Charlie's accident. But I need to look him in the eyes when he says it. See for myself if the guy is lying. Because at this point, he's our only lead. And I want...no, I *need* someone to pay. Need someone to hurt like they hurt Charlie. And if we can't trust the police to do their job, then we'll do it for them.

"His car is here." Tatum nods to the rusted old Taurus in the parking lot. If that was our only lead, I wouldn't feel as confident about what we're about to do. But Tatum is confident that the bastard stole his sweatshirt at the end of football season, and the guy is close to the same height and stature as Tatum.

Plus the asshole is sketchy as fuck.

He was all over Charlie at the stoplight party back in the winter. I wasn't there, but I saw the pictures, and I'd suspected she'd had something slipped in her drink. I should have done something about him then, but I had no proof, and even if she had been given something, there was no way of knowing if it had been him.

I still can't think of a motive, why the guy would have it in for Charlie, but he's got enough strikes against him to make the douchebag my number one suspect. Alibi or not.

"Let me talk," I say as we walk into the building.

Tatum rubs his fist. "Trust me, I don't plan on doing any talking." He wants vengeance as much as

I do, but violence isn't going to help, not until we know he's our guy.

"We need a confession from him." I narrow my eyes at Tatum, hoping it wasn't a bad idea bringing him with me.

"Don't worry, I'll get one." Tatum bangs on the apartment door, hard and continuously, until it opens.

When it opens, Decan looks momentarily shocked to see us, before a snarl tugs at his lips and he spits out, "What the fuck do you want?"

Tatum wasn't lying when he said he didn't plan on talking, the guy barely has the words out before Tatum has pushed into his apartment and has Decan up against the wall. I let him get a few punches in before I stop him.

"Enough," I say, pulling him back by the shoulder.

Decan stumbles when Tatum releases him, but his hard gaze is directed at me. "I'll have you both locked up for this." He runs his tongue over his teeth like he's checking if Tatum knocked any out.

"It's you who's going to be behind bars. Attempted manslaughter, vandalism, stalking," I say, shoving my hands in my pocket and going in for the kill. "Even without any priors, I'm thinking that'll get you at least five years." I let a vicious smirk play on my lips. "You know who I am, right?"

"Yeah, Beckett. I know who you are." There's deep-rooted hate in his eyes. "You're a pathetic excuse for a human. And I'll be there cheering when you finally burn."

It's not a confession, shit, it's not even a motivation, but there's something in his words and the way he's glaring at me that sends out all types of warning bells.

"Then you know my family has the power to lock you up, for a long time."

Decan spits blood. "The police already came here. I have an alibi. You have no proof—"

Tatum moves toward him again, looking ready to beat the proof out of him, but a small gasp from down the hall stops him.

"What's going on?" A skinny blonde, wearing only an extra-large t-shirt, her hair a tousled mess steps out of the bedroom, eyes wide when she looks at Decan and sees his busted-up lip. "Should I call the cops?"

Shit. We hadn't planned on witnesses, and if Tatum does anything else, I don't think even my father's lawyers can get him off.

Decan is still glaring at me as the blonde moves

to his side and he places an arm over her shoulder, using her like a shield against any more of Tatum's blows. "No, they're just leaving."

Frustration blazes inside me, because we're nowhere closer to getting a confession from him. "You said you had an alibi, Saturday night?" I ask, not ready to leave without something.

"He was with me," the girl says.

"Bullshit," Tatum mutters.

"The whole night?" I ask, holding the chick's gaze. I've seen her around campus. I'm pretty sure she's propositioned me more than a couple of times over the years. "You can vouch that he was with you the entire time?"

"Uh, yeah, we were...we were here..." She licks her lips, gaze dropping to my chest, even lingering shamelessly on my groin before pulling her eyes back up to my face and giving me a lascivious smile. "Fucking all night long. My friend Stacey was here with us, you remember her, she's never stopped bragging about having the infamous Princeton Charming. Do you want me to give her a call? I'm sure she'd be happy to meet with you to discuss the details."

I clear my throat and glance back at Decan

whose expression is unreadable other than the hate that's directed at me.

"You want to find the person responsible for hurting your girl, Beckett?" Decan says. "Go look in the mirror."

Tatum takes a step toward him, but I put my hand out to stop him, and say to Decan, "If I find out that you lied to me, that you were involved in this in any way—"

"You'll what, Beckett?" A small grin pulls at his lips. "You threatening me? That's what you do, right? All you rich kids. Toss your daddy's money around and act like you can do whatever you want, get away with anything." He turns his gaze to Tatum. "And what the fuck are you doing with someone like him? He's using you as a goon." He snorts in disgust. "What, are you Princeton Charming's personal thug now?"

"I'm not here for him," Tatum tosses back. "I'm here for Charlotte. You almost killed her—"

"Careful." He clucks his tongue and wiggles his finger at Tatum. "Accusing people without any evidence is dangerous." Then his eyes soften for a second. It's brief, but I swear to god I see guilt there, but it could just as easily be empathy. "Look, I'm sorry to hear about Hayes. I hope she's okay." Then he looks back at me, expression hardening again. "But I'm not the bad guy here."

It's frustrating, and I still despise the guy, but I think I believe him, or at least I believe the sincerity of his statement.

Decan rubs his already bruised jaw. "Now get the fuck out of my apartment before I call the cops."

I meet Tatum's gaze and see the same defeat that I feel. We start to leave, but at the door, I turn and glance over my shoulder, hand on the frame. "Yeah, Decan, that was a threat earlier. For your sake, I hope you're not involved."

Decan just grunts and slams the door behind us.

Tatum is still muttering curses under his breath as we get in the car. "You don't believe him, do you?"

"I don't know. What reason would the girl lie?"

"She's a chick, why wouldn't she?" He rubs his eyes, and mutters, "Fuck. I just want to find the person responsible so we can end this."

"Trust me, I want the same thing. But I'm not sure if Decan is responsible."

He groans. "Then I just punched an innocent guy for no reason."

"I wouldn't say, for no reason." I chuckle. "The

guy's a douchebag. I'm sure he deserved it for something."

Tatum leans his head back and sighs. "So what do we do now?"

"The only thing we can, make sure Charlie's safe."

I've already been away from her long enough, and I need to get back to the hospital. No, what I need is to get her home.

"Someone needs to pay," Tatum says, his voice dripping with venom.

"I know you're angry—"

"Do you?" he asks, cutting me off. "Do you know how angry I am? It's Charlie. *Charlie*. If you love her, you'd do anything to find this fucker."

My jaw tightens. Tatum's passion will get him in trouble, but I'm not playing the same end game as him. I don't want to end up behind bars defending my love.

I want to end up with the girl, sharing a life with her. Not paying the price for it the rest of my life.

It doesn't make me weak, it makes me the kind of man Charlie actually needs. Coming here was a bad idea - and I'm done with those.

From here on out, I'm going to be smart. I want

forever with Charlie, and my emotions aren't going to cost me the one thing I want.

Thankfully, I don't have to wait much longer for Charlie to get her discharge papers.

"You look so much better than you did forty-eight hours ago," I tell her as I push her wheelchair to the town car waiting for us outside the hospital.

She laughs. "You saying I looked like crap?"

I chuckle as I help her into the waiting car. "Your words, not mine."

She smacks my arm. "Next time I almost die, I'll try to look prettier doing it."

I know she's just teasing, but my chest tightens at her words, and my muscles tense. I hold her face in my hands. "Let's not talk about you dying, okay?"

It's still too fresh, the feelings still so raw. I haven't had a good night sleep since the accident, and I don't think I will until she's safe in my arms, in my bed.

Safe.

Protected.

Not sure how I'm ever going to let her out of my sight again.

As we near my house, I warn her. "I know

you've had a long few days, but Daphne and Jill insisted on throwing you a welcome home party."

She cringes. "I don't know if I'm up for a whole thing."

"I know. I told them that, but it's just our friends and your Dad. He's leaving in an hour for the airport, but wanted to see you settled in at my place first."

Charlie nods, understanding. "He's been through so much already. I hate that I put him through this too."

"Hey," I say, wrapping my arm around her shoulder, careful to be gentle with her. "Don't say that. You didn't do anything to anyone. None of this is your fault."

"I know." She bites her bottom lip, tears pooling in her eyes. "But we still don't have any idea who might have done it. They're still out there..."

I know her fear, I feel it too. But I have to stay positive for her. Even though it feels like we're falling down a rabbit hole with no answers in sight. If anything, I feel like we know even less than we did before.

"The detectives are on it," I say, trying to sound convincing. "Running prints and looking for the car.

And I have my own guys working on it. We'll find whoever did this."

"I really thought it was Decan, it made the most sense," she says quietly as the car pulls up to my place.

"Yeah, me too." But his alibi checked out, I even had someone check with the other girl, and she confirmed that she was at his place the entire night. "But you're safe, now. I've got a new surveillance system on the condo, and I've hired a driver and guard for when you need to go to classes, and I can't take you."

"It seems like too much."

"I was thinking about wrapping you in bubble wrap and placing you in a padded room," I tease, trying to lighten the mood. "So a surveillance camera and bodyguard is being pretty lenient in my opinion."

She laughs, resting her cheek on my chest, and says softly, "Thank you, Spencer."

"For what?"

"For taking care of so much."

I tilt her chin so she's looking at me. "I'd do anything for you, Charlie, you know that."

She blinks rapidly. "Stop making me cry."

I can tell she doesn't want to get out of the car,

but everyone is waiting inside. I brush her hair from her eyes. "We should go in. Your dad was making his famous chili and cornbread when I left. Said it was one of your favorites."

That gets a smile out of her. "It is. But honestly, anything is better than hospital food."

When we walk through the front door, there's music playing softly, and Prescott, Tatum, and Jill are waiting for us in the living room. Charlie's face brightens as her friends welcome her home.

I like the sound of that - *home* - this being the place she stays for good. God knows I'm not letting her back in that dorm. But we can discuss that later. Now, we just need to make sure she is healthy and recovering.

Daphne runs into the room dramatically. "Oh my God, Char, I'm so glad you're here. I've missed you *so* much. It's so hard to sleep without you in the same room."

I catch Charlie's eyes as Daphne wraps her in a hug. "I've missed you too Daph," she says generously. I know for a fact she hasn't been losing any sleep over not being with her roommate. The girl is a lot to handle, and I'm surprised Charlie has put up with her as a roommate all these years. But that's my Charlie, patient and kind.

"You look good," Jill says, and Charlie is wrapped in more hugs, even Prescott squeezes her shoulder and says, "Glad you didn't die, Hayes."

"Thanks." She shakes her head at him.

I know the two of them will probably never be close, but I'm glad there seems to be some kind of peace now. And I wonder how much is my sister's doing. There's been a huge change in him lately, and I know it has everything to do with Ava.

"Chili's ready," Daniel calls and we all file into the kitchen where the sweet smell of honey and cornbread greet us.

Georgia, Ava, and Yates help Daniel get out bowls and silverware and I find myself smiling despite all the heartache this week. My place has never felt so comfortable before. So much like a home.

Daniel welcomes his daughter with open arms, and his presence relaxes her in a way no one else can. My chest tightens, considering my own fucked up relationship with my parents. I called them after the accident, expecting them to come to the hospital, but they didn't. I don't know if I'll ever forgive them for choosing brunch with a D.C. Senator and his wife over making sure his own son and his girlfriend were okay. And not just us, their own daughter too. Ava lost all sense of security when that intruder violated her space.

This stalker has shaken all of us up. We're changed, on high alert and assuming the worst is just a phone call away. I hate that, the idea that our isolated Princeton community has lost something.

And we have. But as God as my witness, I will set this right, I will find who did this and make them pay. Somehow.

For Charlie.

For all of us.

I place my hand on the small of her back, my need to be near her at an all-time high.

An hour later, when Daniel has to leave, it's everyone's cue to go as well. Even if it was only friends and family here, Charlie is exhausted.

As she's telling everyone goodbye, I head down the hall to grab some extra pillows for her.

I pause when I pass the spare room, noticing Daphne in there, her back to me. She's in the closet, rummaging through a box. I haven't slept here in days, but Daphne has been staying here since the night of the accident. But what she's looking at isn't stuff she brought with her. It's my shit...or rather, the things I'd salvaged from Ethan's place after he'd died.

What the fuck?

Stepping closer, I cough to get her attention. She turns, forcing a smile when she sees me, photographs in her hand.

"Whatcha got there?" I ask, voice brisk and even I can hear the accusation. But I haven't opened that box in years. Couldn't bring myself to do it.

She shakes her head. "Nothing, just knocked over this box in the closet. I was picking it up and these photos spilled out." She stands, handing them to me when I approach. "This was your brother, Ethan?"

I take the photos, flipping through them. "Yeah, from when we were younger."

"You've been through a lot," she says, her eyes on the photos. "I was an only child, I've always been jealous of people with siblings."

"Ethan was a good brother," I say, trying hard to separate my feelings about the man I remember and the man whose confession on the recording left me reeling.

"You guys look happy," she says, pointing to a photo of Ethan, Ava, and I. It was a Christmas morning and one of the few candid photos I have of us. Most every picture we have together was staged.

I feel bad for my initial reaction.

"I think..." She lets out a shaky breath. "I think I may have misjudged you originally. I'm sorry about that. You seem like a decent guy, Spencer."

"Charlie makes me a better guy," I admit, knowing her first impression of me was probably right. "Thanks for being such a good friend to Charlie. I know all this stuff has been pretty scary."

"I should be thanking you for letting me crash here. My parents will be here tomorrow, so I won't inconvenience you much longer. They're going to get me an apartment in town with a doorman and security cameras. My dad was pretty upset."

"I can imagine. Where do they live?"

"Chicago. My poor mother has been Facetiming me every few hours since this all happened."

I chuckle. "Overprotective mothers are a force to be reckoned with. But I'm glad you have parents to lean on, nonetheless." I set the photos in the box and place the lid on top.

Wishing my own parents were the kind I could lean on.

In fact, wishing my entire family could turn back the clock and start over.

4

CHARLIE

Waking up at Spencer's place is starting to feel familiar. His arms are always wrapped tight around me, his warm body lulling me back to sleep. Which is something I'm finding I'm needing most nights.

I keep waking with nightmares, reliving the accident in my mind. My car skidding off the road, the sound of the crash, the numbing pain as I lost consciousness.

Spencer is always here. "Shh, Charlie, I got you, you're okay."

But am I?

He wipes my tears away, pulling up my favorite songs on his phone, helping me any way he can to rest. It's what I need, what the doctors insist I get more of - but it's hard. How can I rest when I know someone is after me?

Still, I can't stay in his cocoon forever, and after a few days, I know I need to get back to classes. I'm ramping up toward graduation and even though I have been accepted into the master's program, now isn't the time to start dropping the ball.

"You'll be fine," Jill tells me. We're in Spencer's kitchen making dinner together - Chicken Piccata. She's worried that I'm not eating enough.

She isn't wrong. I haven't had an appetite since this all started. "You're strong and capable, Charlie. And knowing Spencer, you'll have a full entourage wherever you go."

"I know, but isn't that a little overly dramatic?" I ask, wondering why I care what anyone else thinks. "Too intense?"

Jill shakes her head as she dips chicken breasts in flour. "No. This isn't a college prank, we know that. Spencer is doing the right thing. Let him."

I chew my bottom lip, draining the boiled pasta in the sink. "You think he's good for me?"

Jill smiles, adding lemon and capers to the sauce on the stove. "It's strange, I never thought I'd be saying this - not in a million years. I mean, I always thought you and Tatum would ride off into the sunset together."

"But?" I ask, reaching for a bottle of white wine and pouring us both hefty glasses.

"But he's won me over. *Charmed* me if you will," she says with a smile. "Yeah, I think he's good for you."

"The idea of dying, of losing him, losing a life with him - it's scary." I blink back tears as she turns to me.

She wipes her hands on a dishrag and pulls me into a hug. "You're not in danger of dying. Okay? You're safer than ever."

I nod, wanting to believe her. The nightmares make it hard to put this behind me.

"Safer than ever?" Daphne asks, bouncing into the kitchen. "Did someone find the stalker?" It's her last night here, tomorrow she is moving into the condo her parents bought her. Bought - as if it's no big deal. That is what it's like when you come from money.

I used to think that is what divided me from so many of the students at Princeton, but I was so wrong. Money doesn't define people, their actions and words do. And this week, after the accident, I have been blown away by everyone's generosity toward me.

Georgia is quickly becoming a solid friend, and Ava and I are closer than ever.

"No one found anyone," I say, reaching for another wine glass so Daphne can join us.

"Yet," Jill adds. "Haven't found him *yet*."

We finish making dinner, and by the time Spencer, Prescott, Ava, and Connery show up, the feast is ready.

"Damn, this looks insane," Connery says, taking in the spread of chicken, pasta, salad, warm loaves of French bread. "You made all this?" he asks me.

I laugh. "No. I was the sous chef, Jill was the head cook tonight."

"She's good at taking orders," Jill says, introducing herself to Connery. "I'm Jillian."

"Connery," he says, taking her in. I can tell he likes what he sees. And who wouldn't? Jill is a confident woman. I think that is one of the things that drew me to her in the first place. Well, that and our love for thrift stores. Connery is taller than her, which is a plus, though he's a pretty solid guy with some extra weight. He could be seen as intimidating, but his bright blue eyes and boyish smile put people instantly at ease.

I know it's dangerous to play matchmaker, but I can't help but think they'd look cute together.

We sit at the table and it feels good, all being here like this. The lemony scents of the chicken filling the air and the rich cream sauce making everyone ooh and ahh with each and every bite.

I relax, my shoulders falling as I sip my wine. Everyone seems to be getting along and wanting to be here together. No drama, just eating, drinking, laughing over Connery's self-deprecating jokes. Spencer rests his hand on the small of my back, a shiver of pleasure running up my spine as he does. I lean into him, needing him close.

"You feeling okay?" he asks softly, tucking a strand of hair behind my ear.

I nod, running a hand over his jaw, kissing it quickly. "Better than I've felt in awhile. I thought this impromptu dinner party was a bad idea, but Jill knew what she was doing."

He kisses my cheek, and I cherish it, feeling so secure with the man I love. He'll do anything to keep me safe. "I'm glad we have so many friends," he says. "It helps being in this with other people."

I feel Daphne's eyes on us, and I sit up, reaching for the bread bowl. But Spencer keeps his hand on my knee and the gesture comforts me.

Right now, he is my anchor. Truthfully, I hope he always is.

But I know it's rude to stay in the love bubble, and so I focus on my long-time roommate. "You ready to move into your new place?" I ask her.

She nods, lifting her glass of wine. "It's going to be strange, not being in the dorm, but it will be nice to have a bigger closet."

Ava laughs, raising her glass. "Here, here!"

We crack up and Ava talks a little about her summer internship in London at a fashion house. "I know it sounds glamorous, but it's a little intimidating," she admits. "I want it to go really well."

"But Whitaker will be there too, won't he?" Prescott says, and I wonder if that isn't a hint of jealousy I hear in his voice.

"Who's Whitaker?" Jill asks.

"Winslow Harrington's little brother," Connery fills in. "He's a little...I don't know...slimy if you ask me."

"No he isn't," Ava says, sticking up for him, pursing her lips and crossing her arms over her chest. "We've been close for years. And he even helped me get the blog posts down over New Year's. He's solid."

"Okay." Connery lifts his hands in surrender.

"Good to know. I just spent a weekend with Winslow, skiing, so I'm a little bitter with the name Harrington at the moment."

"Didn't go well?" Spencer asks, chuckling.

"The weekend? Oh, we did a bang-up job convincing my brother we were together, she's good at pretending." He takes a drink of his wine. "But it's always a show with her. And that's coming from the guy who asked her to put *on* a show. It's kind of exhausting."

"Hey, preaching to the choir, brother," Prescott says, chuckling, which gets him an elbow from Ava.

"Sorry," Connery says, shaking his head. "I know you know all this." He leans back in his chair. "This dinner doesn't feel like a show, though. It's fucking refreshing, to be honest."

I laugh. "It's because the infamous Princeton Charming has learned that us commoners are pretty fun."

Spencer laughs, wrapping his arms around me. Everyone groans as he leans in for a kiss.

"You guys are the cutest," Ava says. "I'm really glad my brother is dating you, Charlie. The annual family weekend in Nantucket next month would be so lame if you weren't there."

Prescott laughs. "Wow, I see where I stand."

"It's your first family weekend too, right?" I ask Prescott. The weekend was brought up yesterday when Spencer's mother called confirming that we were still coming.

Spencer had been livid with her for asking about head counts when I was still recovering, but I talked him down. At least his mother has realized I'm not going anywhere. Fighting with his parents isn't going to help anything.

"Yeah," Prescott says, leaning back in his chair a smirk tugging at his lips. "Though I have crashed the event a time or two. But this is my first official invite." There's a flash of pride in his eyes when he looks over at Ava. "I'm glad they approve."

Spencer half groans, half laughs. "I think I'm going to be the one struggling that weekend. I still can't get over my little sister dating my best friend."

We all laugh, and Jill and Daphne go into the kitchen to grab dessert.

"So is Jill seeing anyone?" Connery asks me, leaning across the table.

"You'd have to ask her yourself." I'm not in the business of setting people up, especially since I mistook Tatum and Jill to be a thing not too long ago. Her love life isn't my business, but I add anyway. "But I'll tell you this, she's one of the good ones."

"Yeah," Connery says with a smile. "I see that."

Later, when everyone is leaving, Spencer and I clean the kitchen. Daphne offers to help, but I want to do something domestic, something regular, with Spencer. So much of this month has been dramatic and intense. I want more of this, casual dinner with friends and drying plates and glasses with the man I love.

What surprises me the most, is that Spencer - this elusive and elite man, seems to want the same thing, with me.

"Why are you smiling?" he asks, his hands soapy as he runs a sponge over a dinner plate.

"I'm just happy. In spite of everything."

He pulls me to him, his wet hands on my face, his lips on my mouth. "I'm happy too," he says. His kiss is sweet, gentle and sincere. My heart swells as he kisses me. I swat him on the butt with the dish towel as he takes the dish from my hand and lifts me onto the counter.

"God, I like kissing you," he says, his hands on my waist, my body awake for the first time since the accident.

"I like doing all kinds of things with you," I tell

him, his hands running under my shirt, my skin prickling as he does. His touch is full of desire, and I kiss him again, harder this time.

His mouth opens and I breathe him in as he stands between my legs. I feel his heat, his length, his want.

I know he feels mine too.

"I love you staying here," he says.

The words send a jolt through me, reminding me that this relationship is moving fast. Faster than I ever expected.

"Me too," I admit, kissing his ear, wrapped up in him.

Daphne walks into the kitchen, and we pull back. "Oh, hey guys, am I interrupting? I was just coming to make tea."

Before we can answer, she begins rattling around in the cupboard, grabbing tea bags, putting a mug of water in the microwave. As it counts down the seconds, she rattles on about the night.

Spencer and I share a knowing look. She lives in her own world.

"Jill and Connery seemed to hit it off, didn't they?" she asks, not remotely registering the private moment Spencer and I had been sharing.

"Seemed like it." I tug my hair into a messy

bun. "What is Connery doing after graduation?" I ask Spencer.

"He's starting his doctorate in the fall," Spencer says.

"Oh, nice," Daphne says. "Isn't Jill doing the same thing?"

"Grad school? Yeah," Spencer says with a sigh, obviously annoyed with Daphne, and trying not to show it. "But she wants to get into politics, not teach."

I lift my eyebrows. "How do you know that?"

Spencer smiles, his hands not leaving my hips. "We got to know one another while you were…"

"In recovery," Daphne offers, smiling. "We all totally bonded, didn't we?"

Spencer's jaw tightens. "It wasn't exactly a campus mixer, but yeah, I suppose we all got closer."

Daphne's tea is ready, and she adds several scoops of sugar to it. "I'm restarting keto tomorrow, so today doesn't count," she says as way of explaining a question no one asked.

"Night Daph," I say as she finally takes the cue and walks down the hall to her room.

I exhale, not wanting to complain.

"I'll love it when she finally leaves," Spencer

whispers in my ear, then he blows hot air against it and I giggle, his breath sending warmth down my spine.

"Me too. She's..."

"A lot."

I kiss him again, loving the way our lives have intersected so tightly. His friends are my friends, mine are his - the things that seemed insurmountable - coming from two different worlds, now seem trivial.

We fit.

"*You're* a lot too, Princeton Charming," I say, my eyes roving down to his groin.

He laughs. "You know it. And when Daphne moves out, I plan on showing you just *how much* I am."

5

SPENCER

"Good morning," Charlie whispers sleepily, snuggling her perfect ass against my morning wood.

I groan, pulling her closer, and burying my face in the nook of her neck, inhaling her scent. Waking up to Charlie in my bed every morning has its perks, especially since Daphne moved out. But the best one is seeing her smile first thing in the morning.

She twists around and wraps her arms around my neck, hazel eyes filled with so much love, and I can't help but suck a breath in. Fuck happily-ever-afters, this, right here, is what everyone should be striving for - to wake up with the person they love and feel like the world makes sense.

Her smile broadens, and I kiss her nose. "What are you grinning about?"

"I'm just happy."

I kiss her, soft, gentle, but it quickly turns into more, and it's not long before I'm buried deep inside her, my own groans matching hers before my thrusts send us both over the edge.

Another perk to having her here.

"Love you, Spencer," she murmurs, her breathing still ragged.

"Remember that when you're stuck in a house with my parents all weekend," I say, remembering what day it is. Ava and Prescott will be meeting us at the airport in a few hours to take the family jet to Nantucket.

"It'll be fun." She presses her lips to mine before rolling out of bed and heading toward the bathroom.

"I think our definitions of fun are slightly different."

Charlie's laughter is followed by the shower turning on. I'm about to follow her and show her the fun I prefer when my cell buzzes on the nightstand.

"Hey Beckett," Sam Paparelli says. He's one of the private investigators I hired after Charlie was run off the road.

"You have anything for me?" So far he's done a shitty job. But then so have the local police. The only thing that's given me confidence is the security team I have watching Charlie twenty-four-seven.

There's a heavy sigh on the other end of the receiver before Sam says, "If I'm going to get anywhere, I need more to work with."

"I've given you everything I have. What about Decan? Have you looked into—"

"I'm telling you, his story checks out. And from what I can tell he doesn't have the skills or the IQ to pull off the advanced coding on those blogs. Plus, if your dates are correct, he wasn't on campus when Charlie got the first note."

I pinch the bridge of my nose, frustrated, but Sam isn't telling me anything I don't already know.

"I can keep working the case, but unless whoever is behind this strikes out again, I really have nothing to go on."

At least the man is honest, even if it's not what I want to hear.

I hang up, and join Charlie in the shower, kissing her hard when I step in.

She blinks up at me, and her small frown tells

me that she's read my mood. "You're really stressed about this weekend, huh?"

I shrug and press my forehead to hers and let my hands roam down her body. I just want her safe, but telling her about my call will only upset her, and she's just starting to finally sleep through the night without nightmares.

"When we're there, any time you want to leave, just tell me. I'll have our bags packed and us out the door before you can—"

"Hey." She smiles up at me. "If we're going to be together, I'm going to have to get used to being around your parents."

"There's no if, Charlie. We are together. Anyone who has a problem with that will have to deal with me."

Her lips twitch up.

"What?"

"I like when you go all alpha protector on me. It's sexy." Her tongue darts out across her bottom lip, and her eyes fill with desire.

I smirk, lifting her up so that her legs wrap around my waist, and my already hard cock is pressed against her. "You keep looking at me like that and we're never going to make it to Nantucket."

She chuckles. "I think Ava and Prescott can wait a few extra minutes."

"Oh my God, this place," Charlie says as our car pulls up to the family home, the place I've spent every summer of my childhood.

"I know, right?" Ava says, blue eyes sparkling. She takes Charlie's arm and starts to drag her toward the house, leaving Prescott and me to gather the bags.

"Hey," Prescott calls out. "A little help."

Ava looks over her shoulder and chuckles. "You two can manage. I want to show Charlie the beach."

The two of them disappear behind the dunes, and Prescott mutters under his breath as he tries to manage my sister's two oversized suitcases, along with his own.

"Jesus," he grunts. "I swear she packed these things with rocks. Who needs this much stuff for one weekend?"

"Ava." I laugh. Thankfully Charlie only packed a small duffle bag, and I'm already halfway up the front steps when the doors swing open.

"Boys." My mom gives me a polite smile before her eyes light up when she sees Prescott. I'm still not in her good books, but I can't bring myself to care. She's not one of my favorite people at the moment either.

"Mother," I say, kissing her cheek when she gives me a stiff hug,

"I'm so glad you made it," she says. "How was the flight?"

"Uneventful," I say. Which is exactly how I'm hoping this weekend will be, but I can already see from the glassiness of my mom's eyes that she's had a few martinis.

"Good, good." She glances around. "And where's Ava?"

"She took Charlie down to the beach," I tell her, aware of the way her mouth turns down slightly when I mention Charlotte.

I'm about to warn her to be nice, but she ushers us inside before I have the chance, and starts, "Your rooms are all set up. I have you boys on the third floor at the end of—"

"Charlotte and I will be sharing a room," I say, holding her gaze.

Her hand flutters to her chest, and her eyes

widen. "That's highly inappropriate. I've put the girls—"

"Mother," I say sternly, not willing to back down, not even for the small sliver of peace I know will come. "I'm sure I don't need to remind you whose name Grandfather put this place in when he passed." It's only a small warning, but it's one that gives her pause.

Much to my mother's surprise, my grandfather left his entire fortune - every single penny - in Ethan, Ava, and my name when he'd died. But the house, this house, was given to me. Even I'm not sure what motivated his decision, but I know it crushed my mother, and since then she's been almost tyrannical about lording over the estate while she still can.

But after I graduate next month, she'll no longer be the trustee over it.

It'll be mine to do with as I please.

My father has wealth of his own, more money than my mother could ever spend, but I know she's still bitter about it.

"Well." Her chin tilts up, expression barely flinching before she turns to Prescott. "We'll be having an early dinner on the terrace in an hour." She gives a stiff smile. "I hope you're both hungry."

"Famished. I've been looking forward to one of your meals all week." Prescott gives her one of his grins, lightening the mood as he uses his charm to compliment my mom and gain one of her rare smiles.

"I prepared white chocolate cranberry cheesecake for dessert. It's one of Ava's favorite."

I grunt, knowing the only thing my mother did to prepare anything was order her servants around. But then, she's always been very good at that.

Leaving the two of them, I head up to the third floor. There's a small bedroom on this landing with the best view. I pause in the hall, a flood of memories crashing over me, stronger than the ocean waves on the beach.

Growing up, this felt like home in ways our D.C. house never did. It was here my grandmother patiently taught me how to ride a bike, where my grandfather taught me to play poker using peanuts, where my sister and brother and I would dig in the sand until our shoulders were sun-kissed and our cheeks had freckles.

It was safe, it was familiar. In the summer, it was long days with sand castles and clambakes. And in the early spring, like it is now, we would ride our bicycles into town and go to the bowling alley and arcade. Our regular, day-to-day lives, even as children, were consumed with elite private schools, tutors, and learning French and Latin. Here though, in Nantucket, we were free to be children.

That was before we lost Grandma and Grandpa.

Before we lost Ethan.

Now, nothing is the same as it was. With my parents running the show, the house feels no different than the place they own in D.C.

Except I have memories here. Memories that bring me back to a simpler time. A time where love and laughter reigned. Where family was everything.

I want more of that.

No matter what I do next, career-wise, life-wise, I want that to be central. To be king. To be the driving force in my decisions.

As I walk down the hall, I pause at the family photos my grandma hung. My grandparents on the beach, walking hand in hand. A photo of my siblings and I on the whitewashed deck, sand dunes and ocean waves behind us, grinning as we waved sparklers on the Fourth of July. A snapshot of the family elbow deep in butter with a table full of lobster claws.

My grandparents had money, loads of it - but

they had something else. Something I have too, something I didn't know I needed until Charlie came into my life.

Love. True, impenetrable love.

I choose a room for Charlie and me, it's not the largest, but it has a large balcony that offers a view of both the sunset and sunrise.

Standing at the window, I watch as Prescott runs down the beach, chasing Ava. I can't hear them, but I can feel their laughter as they roll up their pants and race through the icy water, waves lapping at their ankles and calves.

"There you are," Charlie says, coming up behind me. "You disappeared."

"Do you like it here?" I ask as I pull her to me. She faces out, and we both stand at the picturesque window, the massive ocean stretching for miles.

"It's amazing." I can feel her smiling. "I know I'm supposed to hate this weekend, be a grump because your parents aren't exactly on team Charlie, but I can't let them sour my mood. This place is too perfect."

"I always thought I'd get married here." I feel her stiffen in my arms, but I press on, "I know maybe most guys don't think like that, but I saw a wedding on the beach when I was maybe ten, and I remember thinking the bride and groom, standing on the ocean edge, looked like magic. Glittering sand, blue skies, the whole bit." I chuckle. "Is that weird?"

Charlie looks over her shoulder, her eyes meeting mine. "No, I think it's sweet. You're such a romantic at heart, Spencer Beckett. You hide it well, with the whole manwhore reputation," she says laughing, turning around so we're face-to-face. "But deep down you're sentimental."

"I'm glad you're here with me. The last few years here have been really rough. I think the Nantucket house needed you, Charlie Hayes. To bring some light to a dark place."

She stands on her tiptoes and kisses me. "I love you, Spencer."

"I love you more."

Mom calls us then, and we walk down the stairs, fingers laced. It's crazy, the fact I'm not dreading this dinner. But how could I be? I'll be sitting beside the woman I am absolutely crazy about.

THANKFULLY DINNER IS UNEVENTFUL. Ava and Prescott steal the show by detailing their plans to take a ten-day trip to Australia the week after graduation before Ava moves to London for the summer. They've decided to learn to scuba dive which I find pretty fucking impressive.

"Are you guys going anywhere for end-of-term holiday?" Ava asks Charlie and me.

"We haven't really thought about it," I say. 'We've been really consumed lately."

"I get it," Ava says. "It's been a big month." Then she smiles. "I just like avoiding reality by planning extravagant vacations."

Dad laughs. "You take after your mother in that," he says. "Where are we headed in June, Suzanne?"

"The Seychelles, Geoffrey." She rolls her eyes dramatically. "We've been over it a dozen times."

Charlie smiles at me. "I wouldn't mind coming back here. I'd love to see this place in the summer."

After we eat, Mom retires to her bedroom, and the girls decide to go into town for ice cream. Ava hasn't stopped talking about The Juice Bar since we picked her up to catch our flight, and Prescott agrees to take them. I was going to join them, but my father asked if I would join him for a drink, and I decide to get the conversation over with.

I know he heard about my decision to forgo the

summer internship, and it's no surprise he wants to hash it out. I kiss Charlie goodbye and she leaves the house all smiles. The fact that my parents haven't gotten under her skin yet is no small feat. God, that girl is strong.

My father hands me a scotch, then pours himself one before turning his back on me and heading toward the large bay window that overlooks the beach. He looks tired, and there seems to be more gray in his hair since even the last time I saw him.

I know what he wants to talk to me about. His legacy. The Beckett name. Me following in his political footsteps. Me being more like Ethan. Why I turned down the internship with Senator Johnson.

"If this is about the internship, It's not—"

"I want you to call off your investigator." He turns slowly, blue eyes void of emotion when they meet mine.

I narrow my own eyes at him, suspicion clawing at my throat. "Why?"

He gives a heavy sigh, then takes a deep swallow of the aged, amber liquid before setting the empty crystal glass down. "Because I said so, Spencer."

"Not a good enough reason. Someone tried to

kill Charlie, and I'm going to find out who the motherfucker is—"

"I read the police report, it was an accident."

"An accident?" Anger burns hot inside me. "Someone tried to run her off the road. And it was no accident that both her and Ava's room were vandalized that same night."

He shrugs. "A college prank."

"Are you kidding me? You think it was a fucking prank? Charlie was hurt. Seriously hurt. I thought...I thought I was going to lose her." I slam my glass down on the table, suspicion burning through me. "What are you trying to hide? If you know something—"

"I'm trying to protect you and your sister, and if you want to do the same, I suggest you drop it. Now." He shouts the last word.

In the past, I would have been intimidated by my father. He's a powerful man, and he made certain that his children knew it. And I've always tried to keep the peace. But there's an unease in the back of my skull, a knowing.

It has something to do with the voice recording I got. My brother's confession.

I gave you the fucking money to keep your mouth shut. Don't go having morals on me now. That chick was dead.

There was nothing either of us could do. But I swear to god, that if I go down, you'll go down with me.

"Tell me right now what you're hiding, or not only will I continue my investigation, I'll open it up on you and Ethan—"

"Christ, you always were stubborn." He shakes his head, then sits down in one of the leather armchairs. "You'll make a damn good politician if you can ever focus that hardheadedness."

"You're changing the subject."

"All I've ever wanted..." His eyes close, and I swear I see a tremble go through him. *Fear.* It radiates off him. And there's only one thing that would cause it, he's worried about the Beckett name.

"What did Ethan do?" I ask again, this time slowly, my voice calm, collected, despite the turmoil raging inside me.

"All I've ever wanted was to protect you children."

"Dad." There's a pressure in my chest, making it difficult to breathe.

"It was an accident." He looks out the window, expression stoic, his face a dull, ashen color like all the blood has drained from it.

"What kind of accident?" I ask carefully. There's a part of me that already knows. That knew when I got the phone call. Hell, maybe a piece of me knew even before Ethan drove his car off that cliff.

"He said the girl came out of nowhere." His hands go to his temples. "Ethan said he tried to swerve, but...he called me, and I could hear it in his voice, he was...he'd been..."

I sit down, my own hands starting to tremble. "He'd been drinking?"

"It would have destroyed him. His career. His future."

"What did you do?"

"There was nothing he could have done. The girl was dead. I told him to do the only thing he could."

"You helped him cover it up?" The immorality of the whole thing hits me square in the chest.

"It would have ruined him. Ruined our whole family."

I start laughing, hard, cold, an angry sound that comes from the deepest part of my soul. It's a vicious sound, one full of hatred and rage. When I've collected myself, I stand and pin my father with a look of wrath.

"No," I tell him. "*You* ruined him. *Your* actions destroyed this family."

I start to walk away, but my father growls out behind me. "This is more than a scandal. It's not just me who'll be destroyed if this comes out. Think about your mother, your sister. Think about yourself, Spencer."

I ignore him, needing air, needing Charlie, needing something to take away the open wound in my chest. My father is right about one thing, this isn't just a scandal, it's a crime, and if I expose it, not only will the Beckett name be tarnished, my father could face criminal charges for his involvement in hiding it.

6

CHARLIE

I LAY in Spencer's arms, hear the tumultuous beating of his heart beneath my cheek, feel his rough breaths against the top of my head. Every muscle in his body is tense. The day has only just begun, and he's already stressed out.

Early morning sunlight filters through the curtains and I wish we could fall back asleep, that his worries could be put on hold for awhile longer.

"I don't know what to do, Charlie." His arms wrap tighter around me. "I have my guy looking into the accident. I should have the girl's name by the end of the day."

"And then what?"

"I don't know.... My dad was right, it doesn't just involve me, there's Ava to think about."

I shift so that I can see his face. "You should tell her."

He sighs. "I know. And I will. I just...I need to work through it first."

"What your brother did, taking off, it was wrong, but..." I place my hand on his cheek. "It was an accident."

His jaw bounces under my touch. "Except that he was drunk. It may not be murder, but it is manslaughter. And the girl's family..." He shakes his head. "I think about not knowing who ran you off the road, and what it's done to me. Imagine what they've gone through...not knowing who killed their daughter."

"You are such a good man, Spencer Beckett. I love you so much," I say, pressing a kiss to his chest. "You'll do what's right. I know it."

He takes my fingers and brings them to his mouth. "I just don't know what that is."

"You'll figure it out," I tell him. Believing that with all of my heart. "Maybe you just need to let your mind think about something else for awhile, and then, when you don't expect it, you'll have the clarity you need.

He lifts his eyebrows as I run my fingers over his bare chest. He is a pillar of strength, and his ripped body turns me on, in even the most intense moments.

"How do you suppose I clear my head?" he asks, his eyes catching mine.

I reach beneath his boxers, taking hold of his thick cock. "I have a few ideas," I tell him with a wry smile.

"We have to be quiet. Ava and Prescott are sleeping right below us."

Charlie shakes her head. "Nope, earlier when I got up to get a glass of water I saw them running on the beach."

His hands push down my panties. "In that case, we can be as loud as we fucking want."

I laugh, tossing aside my tank top. Spencer's hands run over my breasts, teasing my nipples.

"I love your tits, Charlie Hayes." He kisses one, then sucking my nipples, getting them hard and excited.

I giggle. "You're so weird." I run my hand up and down his thick shaft, loving the way my body feels when he touches me, explores all of me.

"What do you mean? I'm not weird. I have great taste is all." He nuzzles his face against my breasts, and my pussy aches as he plays with them.

I close my eyes, relishing this morning that is so

simple, so pure. Just Spencer and me, no worries about the rest of the world. Just us. It relaxes me in a way I haven't been since the accident, and I know Spencer must sense it, the way my body is opening up for him as his fingers tease my clit, my pussy wet as he circles my tender spot.

"That feels so good," I moan, rubbing my own hand against myself, using my wetness to stroke his cock, getting him harder with each movement of my wrist.

We're facing one another, on our sides, and my knees open for him so he can finger me more fully. He runs his hand through my hair fiercely, as if claiming hold over me and the need begins to build in me so desperately.

"Fuck me, Spence," I beg. "Make me come really hard."

His eyes go dark, and I know he loves it when I talk like this. Like he is the only man in the world who can pleasure me.

The truth is, it's so sexy, the thought that Spencer is the only man who has claimed my pussy; licked me and sucked me and made me writhe against him. I love that he took my virginity, that he has owned my pussy in a way no other man ever has. Ever will.

My hand stills as I consider that. *Ever will.*

Is that what this is? Spencer and me? The beginning of forever?

"You okay?" he asks.

I nod. I'm a little overwhelmed at the thought, but I don't push it away.

I love Spencer - and not just his cock. Everything about him is what I want in a partner, a lover, a husband.

I blink back the thought, wondering if Nantucket is making me a little delirious.

"Hey, Charlie, did I lose you?" he asks, his hand stilling against my pussy.

I shake my head. "No," I whisper. "I'm right here."

And I am. I'm here for Spencer, no matter what happens next. With his family - their secret. With the stalker. With Spencer's career and my aspirations, and our future.

I'm here for it all.

"Good," he says, rolling over me, his thickness eager and my pussy more than ready. "Because I'm not going anywhere without you."

He enters me, pulsing inside me, deep and hard and my body welcomes it. The pleasure and the pain. Everything Spencer is and was and might be. He is also mine.

I cry as my body releases along with him - not censoring my voice. I don't care who hears me, who sees me, who might think what. I have no doubt where I belong, where my place is - not in Nantucket and not in Princeton or in D.C.

My place is right here, with the man I love.

And I'm not going anywhere anytime soon.

"CHARLIE," Ava hollers to me from the beach, waving. But a second later Prescott has her over his shoulder and is rushing toward the waves, pretending that he's about to throw her in.

I shiver just thinking about how cold the water is.

"Here." Spencer places a quilt over my shoulders, then wraps his arms around me. "You look cold."

"She's not a fragile bird, you know," Suzanne says, surprising me by joining us on the beach. She's been slightly removed all day and I wonder if this is all changing too fast for her. Spencer and me, Ava and Prescott. Her family is shifting and maybe she isn't ready for it.

"I never said she was fragile, Mother," Spencer says coolly. "She just looked chilled."

"Hey," I say, resting my hand on his. "It's okay." He is always so quick to fight with his mother, and I wonder if it was always like this. Always butting heads. Defensive. Unable to see the other's point of view.

I know Suzanne has been awful toward me, but I'm desperate to give her the benefit of the doubt. I don't have a mother anymore. And Spencer and I aren't ending things anytime soon. Which means I want a relationship with Suzanne. Not to replace Mom, but because Spencer's family could be my family one day.

God, I want that so much.

"I'm going inside to pack up a bit," Spencer says. "You okay out here, Charlie?"

"You're not leaving for another few hours, are you?" Suzanne asks.

"Yeah, we have a while before the jet will be here." He frowns slightly, as if not wanting to admit something more. Finally though, it seems his conscience wins out. "Actually, I'm going to look through some old photos, if you don't mind. I'd like some at my townhouse."

I watch as Suzanne's lips press tightly together. "No, that's fine, of course. Take whatever you want."

He squeezes my shoulders before walking away and I can see the torment in his eyes as he leaves. I start to move, thinking maybe he shouldn't be alone, but Suzanne shakes her head. "Let him be. He's like that. Needs space to think things through."

I nod, knowing what she means. Spencer is the sort of person who needs time to process on his own.

Just when I think Suzanne isn't going to say anymore, she adds, "He's the opposite of Ethan, in that."

My eyebrows lift. "How so?"

She sighs, gesturing to a pair of Adirondack chairs in the sand. We sit, the waves ahead of us, Ava and Prescott in the distance. Their incessant laughter mixing with the seagulls flying low. Ava brings out a playful side of Prescott, a side that was sorely hidden when I first met him on campus. He was so callous and crass. Now he seems lighter, like he's taken a breath of fresh air for the first time in years. And Ava is that clarity he needed.

"Ethan was like Ava. Easy-going, not taking anything too seriously. He could make a decision and run with it in the blink of an eye." She doesn't look at me when she talks, but I know her words are for me. "After we lost Ethan, Spencer changed."

"But he is the notorious Princeton Charming," I say. "When I met him, he was the life of the party."

"Was he though?" she asks. Her question surprising me.

"What do you mean?" I know his reputation on campus. How he could flirt his way anywhere, could offer a single smile and have his way with anyone.

"It's not real. Not the real Spencer. Surely you know that by now." She looks at me, assessing me. Wanting to see how deep I might go.

"I always thought he was this playboy on campus," I admit. "So when I finally got to know him I was shocked to see—"

She cuts me off. "That he is actually a good man with a pure heart?"

I smile softly. Spencer may think his mother doesn't understand him, but maybe she knows him better than anyone. "Yeah, exactly that. He is a man who has ambition that reaches farther than power and prestige."

"I know," she says, exhaling. As if the reality is a lot for her to bear.

"Then why are you so hard on him? Pushing him to be something he isn't?"

"The world is a cruel and relentless place, Charlotte. You know that. You lost your mother, recently, and you've been threatened multiple times. You aren't naive."

"Neither is Spencer."

Suzanne nods, then she takes my hand in hers, a gesture that shocks me. Her eyes are glassy - but she hasn't had a drop to drink. "I want Spencer to be on top because I can't bear the thought of him being crushed. The world isn't kind to men with noble intentions."

"It kills him to think you don't see who he really is," I tell her, the words catching on my emotions. "I lost my mom this year. But she died with me knowing her love was unconditional. I don't think your son feels the same way."

She pulls back wiping her eyes. "I hate thinking that you're right," she says. "That he might doubt my love."

"So what are you going to do about that?" I ask, proud of myself for not backing away from one of the hardest conversations of my life. Most unexpected too.

"I suppose I could start with saying that I'm really glad Spencer has a woman like you in his corner." She squeezes my hand again, and I blink back the tears that fill my eyes as I realize this is one of the hardest conversations she's probably ever had too.

"What are you guys talking about?" Ava asks when she and Prescott run over to us, not realizing the moment had been fraught with emotions.

Suzanne stands, clasping her hands together. "We should have some lunch before you head back to Princeton, what do you think?"

Prescott grins. "I can make my famous tuna melts."

"Gross," Ava groans. "I want something good. No offense."

"We could go to Salty's Shack for clams," Suzanne suggests. "It's Spencer's favorite."

"You'd eat there, Mom?" Ava asks skeptically. "You've always said anything deep fried is beneath you."

"Do we have time?" Prescott asks.

I look over at Suzanne. She's trying. In her own way.

"I think Salty's sounds amazing," I say.

Ava claps. "Perfect. Grandpa always took us there as kids," she explains to Prescott and me.

Prescott chuckles. "You do realize I spent my summers on Nantucket too, Ava? My family house is two blocks away."

Ava laughs as we walk into the house, surprising Spencer with the restaurant choice.

He's standing at the kitchen island with a box of photographs. "And Mom and Dad are coming?" he asks with a frown.

Suzanne examines her manicured hands. "Well I'm going, not sure about your father."

"Where'd you find these?" Ava asks, grabbing a pile of pictures.

"In the closet, along with this treasure," he says teasingly, presenting her with an old Monopoly box.

Ava raises her hands the moment she sees the game, her eyes wide and gleaming. "No, way, get that thing away from me."

Geoffrey walks into the kitchen just then, and Ava backs into him. "Why in the world is that game out?" he asks, his expression relaxed for the first time since I've met him. "Last time it was played in this house everyone refused to speak for a week."

I look around the kitchen, everyone is laughing,

reminiscing about Ava's refusal to sell Illinois Avenue and Suzanne's hold on Park Place. Standing here, I see, for the first time a normal family, with inside jokes, and stories that are about things beyond image.

And I realize just how much damage Ethan's death brought to the Becketts. It rocked them to their core, changed who they were. I don't doubt that there were always deep roots, ties to power and money, but maybe it was about more. Maybe Spencer's perception of his family has been clouded by his brother's untimely death. And as we all load into the luxury SUVs to get French fries and clams, there is a knot in my stomach.

They may be making inroads in some ways, but if Spencer moves forward with the information his father gave, all of it will be for naught.

This family will be more than broken.

It will be ruined.

7

SPENCER

"You survived a weekend with my family," I say to Charlie when we're back home, nuzzling her ear, and feeling some of the weight of the weekend fall from my shoulders.

Not all of it. I still have decisions to make. Choices that could ruin the Beckett name.

Charlie grins as she turns around in my arms. "I actually think I made some headway with your mom."

"Really?"

"I'm not saying she likes me, but I think she knows I'm not going anywhere."

"Damn straight, you're not." I pick her up, tickling her as I place her on the bed, my mouth and hands desperate for contact.

"I still have to unpack," she says through a fit of laughter.

"It can wait until tomorrow." I kiss her neck, my hand snaking under her shirt and finding one of her perfect breasts. "I'll have someone pick up the laundry in the morning—"

"I can do my own laundry, Spencer."

We've had this argument a few times and I'm not in a mood to rehash it. "Okay. But if you think for one second, I'm getting rid of the housekeeper—"

She laughs and pulls my face to hers, kissing me. "It's your place, you can do what you want."

I push myself up, holding my weight on my forearms. "It's *our* place, Charlie. You live here too."

She studies me for a long moment, and I expect an argument, but instead, she chews on her bottom lip. I can practically see the wheels spinning, but I don't know what she's thinking.

I tap the line that's formed between her brows. "I know that look. Talk to me."

"I just..." She shifts away from me, and I let her, realizing we're about to have *the talk*, the one I've been avoiding since she moved in here after the accident. "I'm so grateful for you letting me stay, but..."

"You want to move out?" It's what I've dreaded. But I know I can't force her to stay, no matter how much I want her here.

"No." She gives a small shake of her head. "I mean, not unless you want me to."

"Hell, no. I want you here." I take her hand and place it on my chest, over my heart. "I want this to be *our* home."

She swallows hard. "But you still haven't decided what you're going to do next fall. If you move away, I need to start looking for a place—"

"This place *is* yours, Charlie." I hold my breath, not knowing how she's going to respond to what I'm about to tell her. "No matter what happens between us, you never have to leave."

She frowns. "Is something going to happen between us?"

"Shit. No. I'm not saying this right. I just want you to feel like you've got something of your own...So..." I sit up and drag my hand through my hair. "Don't freak out, but I put the condo in your name."

"You did what?" Her eyes go wide, and she pulls back.

"The place is yours. There are a few papers for you to sign, but—"

"Spencer," she bites out. There's the flash anger I expected. "I can't—"

"Before you go off on me, listen. I know what you're going to say."

"Then you know I don't want this." She crosses her arms. "That I don't need you buying me things, or...houses...God, Spencer." Her arms lift in exasperation and she starts to get off the bed, but I grab her hand.

"Don't be upset." I twine my fingers with hers, gently pulling her back to my side. "I just..." Shit, I don't know how to explain why I need her to have this place. I'm not even sure I know why myself. "I just need to know you're taken care of. And before you start in on how you can take care of yourself, I know that."

"It feels like you're giving it to me in case we break up."

"God, no. That's not why." I cup her jaw, willing her to understand my heart. "I wanted to give you something, a piece of me, something we can share...I want you here, in my bed, in *our* bed...I'm screwing this all up."

"So giving me this place is your way of asking me to move in with you permanently?" She's smirking at me now, and her anger is gone. Thank god.

I breathe out a sigh. "Yes. And I'm starting to think it wasn't the best way to do it."

She laughs. "No, a key in a little box with a red bow would have worked much better." She straddles my waist and her arms go around my neck. "So ask me."

I nip at her chin. "Is that a yes?"

"I don't know, depends on the question."

"You're a brat, you know that?"

Her fingers are in my hair, and she smiles down at me with desire, and lust, and love. "I'm still waiting."

"Fine." I grin. "Charlotte Hayes, will you please move in with me?"

"I don't know." She shrugs, then chuckles. "I recently acquired this gorgeous two-story condo, maybe you should move in with *me*."

I swat her ass and laugh. "Nothing would make me happier."

Her mouth crashes down on mine, and my chest swells with the love that emanates from her.

"God, I can't believe we're doing this." Her voice is full of excitement. But I am so relieved to know she feels it's the right thing for her too.

After everything that's happened, all the trials and losses, we're together, and maybe even stronger from it. *Nothing will come between us again.*

"Love you, Charlie," I say, loving the way the words feel on my tongue, how they make my chest constrict with emotions and gratitude.

She kisses me, but our moment is interrupted when both our phones start buzzing at the same time.

I frown as we both reach for the devices. But it's anger and fear that turns my insides to liquid fire when I open my messages and scroll through the link that Prescott sent.

Prescott: I'm already working to get it taken down, but I thought you should see it if you haven't already. Don't worry the fucker will pay for this.

"Oh my god," Charlie says quietly beside me, and I know she's been sent the same link.

It's another blog, this one titled *Cinderella or Skankarella? How to bag (pun intended) your very own prince.* There are photos, but it's the video that has my heart beating wildly in my chest, praying it's not what I think it is.

Charlie has already clicked on it, and the sound of her moans come from the small speaker and my own voice as I fuck her slightly distorted from the choppy video.

"Fuck. I'm going to kill the bastard..." I take her phone from her hands, and turn it off, but not before getting a good glimpse of the room we were in - our bedroom in Nantucket.

Someone recorded us while we were there on the weekend.

"Who...who would do this?" Charlie asks the question we've been asking for months. And I still have no answers for her.

She's shaking violently when I pull her against me. I can't even tell her it's going to be alright, because nothing is all right about it.

What the actual fuck?

But my question is no longer who the hell would do this, but who the fuck had access to that bedroom.

8

CHARLIE

I can't stop shaking and my hands feel like they've gone numb, my lips too.

Spencer is shouting at someone on the phone, but my thoughts keep replaying the video of Spencer and me over and over again.

"Just get the fucking video taken down," Spencer yells before hanging up and tossing his phone across the room. It hits the wall, and I jump slightly at the sound. I know I should be just as angry, but I feel...violated. Dirty.

How many people have already watched the video? Even if it gets taken down, the damage is already done. And it's not just my own reputation, it's also Spencer's. The sex tape could ruin his chances at a political career in the future.

And we're still no closer to finding the person responsible.

But something presses at the base of my skull, like some important fact that I'm missing.

"I want to see it again," I whisper.

"What?" Spencer stops his pacing and looks over at me.

"Give me my phone. There was something I missed."

Spencer frowns and hesitates before pulling out my phone from his back pocket.

I scroll past the video and study the pictures that were posted beneath it. One catches my eye, and I stop, staring at it, knowing there's a clue in it.

It's a photo of Spencer and me on Valentine's day, we're inside the old record shop our heads close together, obviously deep in conversation.

"What is it?" Spencer asks, sitting beside me.

"I don't know. I just..." And then I see it, the reflection in the glass. I magnify the picture and suck in a small breath when I see the distorted, but familiar face. It's unfocused, but there's no doubt who it is. "Winslow."

Spencer grabs my phone from my hands, anger blistering off him. "Christ. What the actual fuck?"

Part of me doesn't believe it. But there's no

doubt that it's her in the photo. The blonde hair, the red Burberry jacket with the silver pendant she always wears. "It's her. She's the one who took the photos...who recorded us."

There's not even a moment of hesitation from Spencer, he's back on the phone, ordering someone to blow the photo up. Then he's calling his parents, demanding who had access to the Nantucket house before we arrived. After his mother confirms that Winslow and her parents had stopped by the weekend before, Spencer looks like he's about to lose his mind.

"I should have known it was her." He's pacing again, his face bright red, and if we were in one of those old cartoons, there'd be smoke coming out of his ears.

"She may have been responsible for the blog, but she wasn't driving the Taurus that night," I say. "It was a man. I'm sure of that."

"Yeah, maybe. But she can't get away with this." Spencer shakes his head, looking as overwhelmed as I feel. "I'll deal with her."

I thought I'd feel relieved when I found out who was responsible, but I just feel...raw.

"It has to be me," I say. "I need to confront her."

"No." Spencer's nostrils flare. "I don't want you anywhere near her. She's insane..." He takes a deep breath, then growls out, "When I'm done with that bitch..." He inhales through his nose and I swear he's going to crack his teeth with how tight he clenches his jaw. "I'm going to ruin her."

"Spencer." I stand and place my hand on his arm, feeling oddly calm. "I need to do this. If it's you, she'll always think that I'm weak, that she can walk all over me."

"No."

"I'm not asking you."

"I promised to protect you." He drags both hands through his hair, making it stand on end. "This is my fault. I should have realized what a spiteful, toxic—"

"It's not your fault." I lean up and kiss his cheek.

"God, how can you be so calm right now?"

"Trust me, I'm as angry as you are. But I have a plan. We can't erase what she did, but we can make sure she knows never to mess with me again."

The Ivy is packed when we walk through the

doors. Heads turn and the whispers and laughs start. I was ready for this, but I'm grateful for Spencer's hand that rests on my lower back, fueling me with strength.

I can do this.

I'm not a fighter. I've never thrown a real punch in my life. And I'm not going to start now, no matter how much the woman deserves it.

But I'm also not going to let Winslow Harrington have the last word. Not when her choices violated every girl code ever created.

"You sure you want to do this?" Spencer leans down and asks against my ear.

I nod, pulling out my phone and setting it to record. I want to pick up every single word Winslow mutters as she tries to dig herself out of the hole she dug with her own two backstabbing hands.

"I've never been more sure of anything."

At least that's what I think before I enter the lounge where members of the elite club are hanging out. Yates, Prescott, and Connery lift their hands in greeting when they see us, but Spencer just nods and keeps walking straight ahead.

"I got this Spencer, go talk to your friends," I say. I love him, but I need to deal with this on my own. "I want to fight my own battle this time."

"You can't trust her," he warns.

"I know that."

"I'll be right over there," he says, running a hand through his hair. "If you need me."

I walk to the far corner where Winslow is holding court. She has a glass of champagne in hand and is talking with a group of women. Georgia is with her. My stomach rolls. Is Georgia in on this too?

But when Georgia sees me, she waves me over, her smile genuine.

It's now or never.

Georgia stands, giving me a hug. "Hey sweetie, it's been a few days. How are you?"

Obviously she hasn't seen the blog or the video. Thank god, I'd thought the whole school would have seen it by now.

Winslow snorts, blue eyes scanning me, a look of disgust pulling her lips up and distorting her pretty face. "Are you serious? You're like friends or something?"

Georgia bites her bottom lip, shrugging and I realize she hasn't told Winslow that we've been hanging out at all, going on double dates, and getting to know one another. She's terrified of her and for good reason.

"Actually, yeah," Georgia says, looking between us, and I see when she makes the choice to stand up for herself. She straightens and her chin lifts. "Yates and Spence go way back, and we've all been—"

Winslow cuts her off. "*We* go way back too."

"I know, but Winnie…" Georgia lowers her voice and I stand there fuming, waiting to strike, ready to expose her for the vicious viper she is. "But, it's not like she did anything to you. I don't know why you have to be so…mean."

Winslow glares at Georgia. "Are you fucking stupid? This slut stole Spencer from me."

There is a collective intake of breath and I just can't get why Winslow won't let this all drop. People break up all of the time. Why is she so obsessed with my boyfriend?

"Winnie," Georgia says, looking around.

There are more than a dozen heads turned in our direction now, watching, waiting. They want a show, and Winslow seems content on giving them one.

Georgia says softly to her, "Let's not do this, here. Maybe we should go somewhere more private."

"Or maybe she needs to leave." Winslow glares

at me. "You don't belong here, Cinderella. Unless you're mopping floors or washing dishes."

"Winnie," Georgia gasps. "Stop being such a bitch."

"It's okay, Georgia," I say, giving her a small smile and trying to hold back my anger. I need to stay calm if I'm going to get Winslow to confess. "Thanks though. But I actually came here to talk to Winslow."

Georgia nods and she hesitantly walks away, but Winslow and I stare at one another, standing face-to-face.

"Why would I want to talk to you," Winslow spits out. She has no clue that I know. She's so caught up in her own delusions that she thinks she's untouchable, which will make her fall all the harder.

"Here's the thing, Winslow." My phone is in my hand, recording. And I know what I have to say, to catch her. "I'm just trying to figure you out."

She purses her lips. "Figure what out, exactly?"

"Why you're so insecure and afraid of other people's happiness. Why you're terrified of me. But most importantly, why you're such a malicious bitch," I say sweetly, lifting an eyebrow. I may have not got into any fist fights growing up, but my father taught me to defend myself. *Stay smart. Stay safe. Stay sassy*. And words are the most powerful thing any of us have. I know the word I used to describe her is evocative - but Winslow slandered me across the internet.

I can't let her get away with this.

"You can call me a bitch all you like Hayes, but at least I'm not a slut."

The crowd around us moves closer, hanging onto every word we exchange. Let them watch. I don't care. I just want Winslow to leave me the hell alone. Need her to confess her part in this.

I see Spencer out of the corner of my eye. He's asking if I need back up, but I shake my head. I have this under control.

"I'm not a slut, Winslow. I'm a girl who is in love with a boy. And like it or not, he chose me. So stop posting about it on the Internet. Stop tormenting yourself for the life you didn't get."

She scoffs, but I see the first hint of fear in her eyes. "I don't know what you're talking about."

"I'm talking about the blog posts. About your hateful words, and your creepy infatuation with a boy who broke up with you."

She narrows her eyes at me, but I see the crack in her veneer, her shaking hand holding the champagne glass and the pursed lips that hold her true thoughts at bay.

And here's the thing. No one does what she did to me unless she truly hates herself.

I look at her, poised, polished, outwardly so damn perfect. But inside? Winslow is a broken girl. They say that real queens fix one another's crowns, but Winslow didn't get the memo.

And as much as she has tried to ruin me, I refuse to ruin her.

I pull out my phone and stop recording. "I was going to tape this all. Me revealing everything you did. Telling everyone here and everyone on campus exactly what you did to me, if they hadn't already seen it for themselves on your blog."

I shake my head looking around the room, at the rich Ivy Leaguers who were fed with a silver spoon, who vacation in the South of France and drive cars that cost more than my father has ever made in a year. I used to hold it against them. Their wealth. Their trust funds and their futures.

But I don't anymore.

Because none of this defines them.

I thought I had learned that already, after the accident, but standing here, finally confronting the person who has done everything she possibly could to make my life a living hell, I am learning the lesson all over again. We are the sum of our actions. Rich or poor, we choose who we become.

Winslow is shaking now, but her gaze is still on me, filled with hate and vengeance that I'll never understand.

"When you do things like this," I say, pulling up the screenshot I took of the blog post, facing it out for her. "You're only hurting yourself. Did you think you'd never get caught? We know you posted the pictures, the video."

"Wait," Georgia says, approaching us. "Is that you, Winnie?" she asks, pointing to the image on my phone. It's the one of Spence and me in the record store.

"I..." Winslow's face has gone white and she sets her glass on the table, looking ready to bolt.

Georgia rips the phone from my hand, her eyes wide. "Winnie, is that you?" she asks again, her voice is high. She's stunned, shocked as she looks at it. It's the zoomed in image and Winslow's signature blonde hair and red coat, next to the full image. "Win, did you...oh, god..."

Winslow begins to back away. "I didn't do anything. I never...I mean—"

"Mean what?" Spencer asks, stepping closer.

And I don't push him away. He needs to confront her just as much as I did. I said my piece, I made my choice. Now he can make his. "You didn't mean to videotape my girlfriend and I in Nantucket? You didn't mean to write fucked up shit and post it all over the goddamn Internet? What's your problem?"

Winslow may put on a tough act with me, but Spencer draws out a different side of her. Tears fill her eyes. She's been caught, and she knows it.

"What's my problem?" she asks, her voice rasing several octaves. "That's what you want to know? My problem is that you and I were supposed to be together, Spencer. So yeah, I wrote the stupid blog, but no one cares. They all know it's the truth anyway. Charlotte Hayes is a money grabbing whore. And she's not good enough for you."

There are gasps around us as she shows her true colors.

"And you are?" Spencer chokes on the words, looking at her evenly. "We've been over this. We were never going to get together after you fucked my brother."

Whispers start.

"Spencer," I say, not wanting to cause more damage than necessary.

"I fucked him to make you jealous," she says,

hysterical now. She looks like a wild animal caught in a cage, her eyes darting from Spencer to the door, her words spilling from her. "I didn't know he was going to kill himself over it."

"There's a lot you don't know, Winslow," Spencer says reeling. "And since you have no fucking clue about any of it, stop. Now. Or this information won't be kept between friends. Charlie is a better person than me. I'll tell the goddamn world what you did to us."

"Um," Georgia pipes up. "Kinda too late for that."

"For what?" Spencer asks.

"To keep this story between close friends."

I look around the room, realizing everyone is glued to their phones.

Georgia hands hers to Winslow. It's a live feed - someone is recording us minute by minute and posting it to social media.

Everything she just said will never be erased.

"Who is doing this?" she screams. "Stop recording me. Now. Stop it!" She's hysterical, running around the room grabbing at peoples' phones, trying to find the mole.

I pull up the site, whoever is taping this is zoomed in on Winslow as mascara runs down her face. Each time she yells there are more viewers watching as this fallen princess loses more than her tiara. She is throwing away every last shred of her dignity.

I can't watch it - her fall.

I take Spencer's hand, dragging him from the room. Georgia calls after me, saying she is so sorry, that she had no idea. And I know she didn't.

We're in Spencer's car, driving away when the recording finally ends - whoever was taping it finally decided to end her misery.

Then Spencer gets a text:

SORRY FOR HOOKING up with your little sis without telling you.

I know I've been a dick more times than I can count.

But I hope that live performance helped clear my name in your eyes.

Love you, bro.

And love that girl of yours too.

I have your back - always.

--Prescott

9

SPENCER

When we get back to my place, Charlie is buzzing with adrenaline, and so am I. I wanted Winslow to realize the pain she had caused, to have an understanding of just how despicable her actions were, and seeing her go batshit at the Ivy was something I never thought I'd live to see.

"She'll never set foot in there again," I say, grabbing two beers from the fridge as Charlie pops us a bag of popcorn in the microwave. We're having a low-key movie night, just the two of us. We turned off our phones and are going off the grid. After all the drama on campus, we want to spend the night off the radar of anyone.

"Do you feel bad?" she asks, pouring the

popped kernels in a bowl. "That footage is really rough."

I smirk. "Did you already forget what she did to you? Calling you Sluterella, recording us in bed? She doesn't deserve our sympathy after what she did to you."

"I know, she was awful to both of us. I've never felt so violated." Charlie grabs some napkins and we walk to my basement where I have an in home theater. We sit on a leather couch and I turn on the television. "I still can't believe she slept with your brother when you were dating."

"Yeah, it was shitty. But, if she was trying to make me jealous it didn't work. It just disgusted me. We were over long before she did that. I think I always knew what kind of person she was, I just didn't want to believe it. She's been a part of my life for so long."

"I'm not trying to make excuses for her, but what she said about feeling guilty, thinking she drove Ethan off the cliff because she was using him. That's got to mess with a person's head."

"Winslow's head was messed up before that." I run a hand over my jaw. "But yeah, I think that might be part of it. I think she actually loved him in her own fucked up way. Ethan had this way about him." I shake my head, remembering how much I wanted to be like my older brother. How I used to put him on a pedestal. "You think I was a womanizer, well Ethan was more notorious than I was. He was the original Princeton Charming. The king of the campus. He knew how to get what he wanted, at any cost."

"Meaning you think he was using Winslow too?"

I nod. "Except now we know he was dealing with a shit ton of emotional baggage at the same time. They were probably using one another."

"I know she was horrible, but it makes me sad for her," Charlie says, grabbing a handful of popcorn.

I groan, pulling her legs into my lap. "Can we not spend the entire night talking about my ex-girlfriend?"

She tosses a kernel at me, and I open my mouth in time to catch it. "I know, I'm done. I just had to get it out of my system."

"I'm just glad she won't write any more shit about us," I say, squeezing her thighs. "By the way, you were pretty fucking badass, you realize that? Most people are terrified of Winslow, but you held your ground. It was pretty fucking impressive."

"I was just sticking up for myself." She swipes the remote from my hand. "Gimme that, I'll choose the movie."

"Bossy," I tease. "I like it." I take a drink of my beer before setting it on the coffee table, as she begins to scroll through movie options. "I realize you want to change the subject and talking about yourself isn't something you love to do - but I mean it. You were so incredible today." Charlie's cheeks flush and I pull her toward me. "You were strong and yet your heart was in such a good place that you were never cruel."

She shifts and straddles me, giving me one of her smiles that lights up her whole face. "You were pretty badass too."

"Don't make this about me."

"But you were," she insists. "You were my knight in shining armor today, stepping in and helping finish the fight once and for all."

"I think you're the hero of your own story, Charlie." I kiss her, my hands on the small of her back as I draw her to me. In her blue jeans and white t-shirt, she looks so wholesome and sweet, but her kiss tells a different story.

I've corrupted my princess. One kiss and I woke a passion inside her that is comparable to my own.

"You sure you wanna let me pick the movie?" she asks, mischief in her eyes, and something naughty. God, I love her.

"What did you have in mind?"

She licks her lips, pointing the remote at the Pay-Per-View channel. "Something like this?"

I see what she's picked. It's called a *Passionate Flick*. I chuckle. "You know what that is?"

She nods. "I've read the book," she says. "It was pretty hot."

"When do you read romance novels?" I ask having only ever seen her reading textbooks.

"There's lots you don't know about me. Now you'll learn all my dirty little secrets since we'll be living together."

I chuckle. "If this is the kind of dirty secret I can look forward too, we should have started shacking up a long time ago."

"Oh?" Her smile is contagious as she presses play on the movie. "You like the idea of your girlfriend reading steamy stories?"

"How steamy?" I ask.

"Really, really steamy." When I cock an eyebrow at her she giggles. "Well, I had to do something to take care of myself. After all, I was a twenty-two-year-old virgin when we met. What did you think I did?"

My cock stiffens, thinking about her getting off, her fingers teasing her creamy slit, climaxing with her hand. "You'd lie in bed at night and get off while Daphne was in the other bed?"

She rolls her eyes, pressing her hands to my chest, still straddling me. "No. And for your information, Daphne was out a lot, which meant I could do what I pleased. And when she wasn't, I'd go take a shower with my waterproof toy."

I almost choke on the piece of popcorn I put in my mouth. "Your what?" I take a harder look at my girlfriend, not having pegged her as a girl who...well, I don't know what. I just never thought about it before.

"My vibrator." She's smirking at me, I can tell she's enjoying getting me flustered, her words turning me on.

I groan. "God, I'm getting so hard."

"The movie that sexy already?" she asks, rolling off me and facing forward. The main characters are in bed together, naked and just about to fuck. That happened fast.

I laugh, reaching for my beer to wash down the kernel that's stuck in my throat. "No, not the movie.

You. This conversation. Picturing you with a vibrator."

"I have a dildo too."

I spit out my beer. "God, you are just full of surprises."

"I can keep going if you want." She winks. "I have lots of surprises."

I set down my beer and raise my hands. "By all means."

She wiggles her eyebrows as the actress on the screen begins stroking the actor. But we don't need this movie to get in the mood. Charlie is on her knees, unbuttoning my jeans. Her hand pulls out my thick cock and she licks her lips. "This looks yummy," she says.

I shake my head, grinning. "What has gotten into you?"

She shrugs, then teases my tip with her tongue. "It was exhilarating, taking control of our life like that, at the Ivy."

"Our life. I like the sound of that." I run my fingers through her hair. "God, I love you, Charlie Hayes."

"Then stop talking and let me get to work."

"This is work?" I tease.

"No," she sighs. "This is bliss."

She takes me in her mouth, sucking me so damn good. My cock is hard and pulsing as she works her magic on my rod. Her fingers play with my balls, her eyes close and I watch her, loving the way she looks as she gets me off. So innocent yet so damn naughty. Charlie is everything I could ever want in a woman, a partner, a wife.

The thought sends a nervous buzz of energy through me. I never considered getting married so young, but when I look at Charlie, I can't imagine my life without her.

Still, there will be plenty of time for that. She has grad school, and I still have to decide what I want to do about my own career. But, right now I need to concentrate on this night. Not plan out our future.

Charlie's eyes open as my cock thrums with come. "Come here, baby," I say, wanting my girlfriend to sink down against my cock as I come.

She slips off her clothes, her panties, and I pull her into my lap. Her pussy is slick and eager and *mine*. I run my hands over her bare ass as she sits down on me, right where she belongs.

"God, your pussy is tight," I moan. "It feels so fucking good."

She rocks her hips and I pull off her top,

needing her big round tits in my face. I pull her nipple into my mouth, my cock raging and ready as I do. When I come inside her, it's hard and fast and when she moans, her hands on my shoulder, I know there is a need in both of our eyes - for more.

"Do you have your vibrator here?" I ask, wanting to give her every ounce of pleasure I can. Plus, the thought of watching her make herself come makes my balls tighten, my cock harden again.

Charlie nods, licking those luscious lips of hers. "Wanna see it?"

I nod, needing her spread out for me so I can fuck her until we are both panting for breath.

"One sec," she says, bare naked and bounding up the stairs. I move the coffee table aside, dim the lights, turn off the movie, and pull up a playlist I know she likes. When she comes back in, her breasts bouncing as she moves, I begin stroking my cock. I'm already hard as hell and ready to fuck my girl again.

"Okay," she says, her hand behind her back. "Now, I have a few choices, so you get to pick what hand. Right or left?"

I grin, stepping toward her. "Left."

She chuckles. "Good choice," she says,

producing a pink vibrator, her confidence so damn sexy. "Maybe the movie wasn't the right thing to watch, but this is." She sits on the couch, spreading her knees, turning on the vibrator and pressing it to her wet slit.

"My god, Charlie," I groan. My cock is hard, and I step closer to my girl, watching as she gets herself off.

It's hot, so fucking hot. Her eyes close as she moves the wand over her pussy, her fingers circling her clit. I kneel before her this time, my hands massaging her thighs, and she whimpers with delight. "God you're sexy," I tell her.

She moans, her back arching, the vibrator buzzing as she gets herself off.

I kiss her, pulling her mouth to mine, hard. Needing to taste every sweet thing about her. She writhes against me as I kiss her, pulling her to the floor. The vibrator forgotten as she straddles me. Her eyes are fueled with heat as she rides me, our fingers lacing, our bodies one.

When she comes again, it lasts a good long time. I roll on top of her, pinning her to the floor. "God, I'm glad you've moved in."

She nods, then says playfully, "Me too. Because I now have a live-in fuck toy."

My eyes widen, laughter escaping us both. "God, you are so unpredictable. The things you say…" I shake my head.

"I love you, Spencer Beckett." She grins, her expression softening. "And you're more than a sex toy - you're my everything."

10

CHARLIE

"Wait, you've never been to Target?" I stare at Spencer like he is an alien from another planet.

Spencer laughs, reaching for the coffee canister. "Oh shit, we're out of coffee."

We're spending the day moving the rest of my stuff in. Not that I have much, a lot of what I did own had to be tossed after it was doused in pig's blood.

But I enjoy setting up the townhouse for the two of us. It will no longer be bachelor pad central. It'll be *our* place. I'm still not sure about Spencer putting it in my name, but I know his intentions were meant to be sweet, and I no longer want to deny him the need to take care of me ,and protect me. Because I know in my own way, he needs me just as much as I need him.

"We can grab coffee on the way," I tell him as I throw my banana peel in the trash and take the last bite. My appetite is back now, and the nightmares have stopped.

"To Target?" He says, lifting a brow. "You know we can order anything you want online."

I chuckle. "That defeats the whole purpose."

"The purpose is buying shit."

"You've clearly never had the Target experience. I really can't get over the fact you've never been there." I let him help me with my jacket and we head out the door. "Sometimes I forget how different our lives are."

In his car, he plugs the address into his GPS. "So what exactly are we getting there?"

"Not sure. I'll know once I see it."

He shakes his head, laughing, and says sarcastically, "That makes sense."

I swat his arm. "It's the best place for throw pillows, candles, and well, basically a cart full of stuff you never knew you needed. Trust me."

He chuckles as we turn into the drive-thru of a coffee shop. "One Americano and one—" He looks over at me to place my order.

I lean over him and speak into the intercom. "I'll have a nonfat, double tall, half vanilla, vanilla mocha...oh, and don't forget the whip."

"That will be eight dollars and fourteen cents at the window," the barista tells us.

Spencer pulls forward. "Your coffee is over five dollars?"

I pull out a ten dollar bill. "My treat, but yes, I have expensive coffee habits. I guess we haven't really done a lot of normal boyfriend-girlfriend things, have we?"

Spencer waves my money away. "Yeah ,we've been too busy catching stalkers, dealing with grief, losing jobs, hospital stays—"

"Yeah." I cut him off, frowning, knowing there's still a shadow hanging over us. Because even though Winslow confessed to creating those posts, she wasn't the one driving the Taurus that night, and I doubt she'd have had enough strength to throw a rock through my window. "Everything has been so...dramatic..."

"I'm glad we can do normal things now," Spencer says, handing his debit card over to the barista at the window, then turns to me and winks. "Even if it means spending an afternoon at a megastore."

I nod, but I can't help the frown that tugs at my lips as I let my thoughts drift back to that terrible night.

Spencer hands me my drink. "Hey. You okay?"

"Yeah," I say, shaking the memories away, then grin, wanting today to just be about Spencer and me, with no talk about stalkers, or Winslow, or anything else that has tried to get between us. "I think I need to buy a cute pillow, or two, to make me feel better."

He chuckles. "Good thing we're going to Target then." He glances at me from the corner of his eye as he pulls up a playlist. "And you're wrong, Charlie. We don't just do dramatic things. Last night was pure fun. Not to mention sexy as hell."

"It was." A huge grin pulls at my lips as I remember how naughty I was, how liberated I felt. I was nervous to bring out my toys with Spencer, but he loved playing with them. With him, I feel like I can be myself, that I can trust him with even my wildest fantasies - which all revolve around him.

"What are you smiling about?" he asks as we drive toward the shopping center.

"I was remembering last night."

"It was a good movie," he says deadpanned.

"So good," I agree, playing along. "The climax was thrilling."

"And stimulating."

"The plot got going really fast."

He chuckles. "It was hard, real hard. But the ending? Damn, I saw it coming a mile away."

When we get to Target, we're both laughing so hard we're crying and when we get out of the car, he pushes his hand in my back pocket. Keeping me close. Claiming me. I'm h*is*. And I like it.

Because he's mine too.

Coffees in hand, we push the red cart through the aisles, and I grab some throw pillows.

"Really, pink pillows?" He grimaces.

I bite the corner of my lip. "How about seafoam green? Everything you own is grey, this will look nice against it."

"I don't know what seafoam is, but I can handle green." He kisses my cheek. "And we need some cozy blankets to match."

I laugh. "Did Spencer Beckett just say *cozy blankets*?"

He elbows me playfully. "What? I'm not ashamed to say I like to cuddle with my girlfriend."

I twist my lips, my smile probably growing

obnoxious to other shoppers. Spencer and I are in a love bubble and it is impossible to suppress.

By the time we get to the register, the cart is full of lavender dish soap and scented candles. A little dry erase board for the kitchen where we can write down notes for one another. And I got a cute framed print with the quote, *Fight for the fairy tale, it does exist.* I plan on hanging it over our bed.

Our bed.

A rush of endorphins run through me. I still can't believe this is my life.

"Let's grab lunch before we go home," Spencer says as we leave the store with armfuls of bags.

Soon we are at a cafe, ordering at the counter. We slide into a little corner table on my favorite street in town.

"So I've been wanting to talk to you…"

"About what?" I ask, smiling as the waitress brings us our salads and sandwiches.

"I think maybe you should stop working."

I pick up my ham and cheese. "Why?"

"So you can focus on other things. The master's program is hard enough."

"I don't know." I take a sip of water. "I've been working since I was sixteen."

"I get that - and it's so impressive. Your work

ethic is amazing, Charlie. But you don't need the money anymore."

I exhale. "I appreciate the Target shopping spree today, but I need to help with costs. I mean, even if you cover the house, I need money for like...tampons and birth control and to go get drinks with Jill." I smile as I make my point. "To buy new underwear and bras."

"I can buy that for you, Charlie."

I shake my head. "Wouldn't that make me exactly what Winslow accused me of? A money grabber?"

Spencer leans across the table, taking my hand. "I love you. I want to take care of you. Let me."

I still hesitate.

"I have plenty of money. Let me spend it on you."

It's a lot to accept, but at the same time, I don't want to be the girl I used to be. With such a chip on my shoulder, I wasn't able to accept the good things life gave me. I have nothing to prove, and Spencer knows that. He wants me just as I am.

"Okay, but under one condition," I say.

"What's that?"

"We go to the record store after this and pick out some new music. Together."

"Deal." He sits back, smiling. "And I have a condition too."

"What's that?"

"You and I are going to Nantucket this summer."

"For how long?"

"Two months. If you aren't working, you can't fight it."

I shake my head. Two months in Nantucket seems like heaven. "You drive a hard bargain."

"Is that a yes?"

"It's a yes, Spencer Beckett," I say, thinking that my entire life is falling into place.

11

SPENCER

"This is everything?" I ask Sam as I flip through the manila folder he brought over, my chest constricting as I take in the photos of the young woman wearing a Princeton hoodie making fish lips at the camera, another one with her arms around two girlfriends, and the last one of her at her high school graduation with her parents.

"Her name was Shannon Michaels. Pretty sure that's your girl," Sam says as he skims through the envelope of money I toss him. "She was eighteen, a freshman at Princeton when she was killed in a hit and run three years ago."

I rub the back of my neck as I flip through the information Sam collected. She was the valedictorian of her graduating class in high school, and like

Charlie, she was a scholarship student from a blue-collar family.

I remember it now. There hadn't been much media attention at the time, but I recall hearing about it briefly. A small memorial had been set up, with a gathering of students singing songs and lighting candles at the scene of the accident. I hadn't cared much at the time. Sure, it was brutal and unfair, but I hadn't known the girl.

Hadn't known that it was my brother who killed her.

"Want to tell me why you're looking into her case?" Sam asks.

"No," I say, dismissing him. "I'll call you if I need anything else."

I don't get off the couch as he leaves. My head is spinning, emotions choking me. The girl had her whole life ahead of her, and it was snuffed out because my brother had been reckless. Worse, he'd run away like a coward.

"Damn it, Ethan, what were you thinking?" I lean my head back on the couch and close my eyes, my brother's haunted eyes the only thing I see.

I get it now. The late-night phone calls when he'd been so intoxicated or stoned that I couldn't make out what he'd been saying. He'd killed the girl, but that wasn't what killed him. It was shame, remorse...guilt. They were the noose around his neck. If I'd had any doubts before that he drove his car off that cliff on purpose, they're gone now.

"Fucking coward," I grit out, fingers curling into fists. But it's not just my brother I'm angry with, it's the man who helped him hide his crime. The man who was supposed to teach us morals and decorum. It's as much Ethan's sin as it is my father's and I know what I have to do.

"Hey." Charlie's smile falters as she comes into the room. "I thought I heard someone. You okay?"

I push the folder toward her. "My guy brought this over."

Charlie picks it up and flips through the pages, sitting beside me as she does. She doesn't say anything when she closes it, just studies me, waiting.

"I have to tell them." I take her hand and she gives a small nod. "Fuck." I close my eyes again, hating this, but knowing I'll never be able to live with myself if I don't do the right thing. "They live forty minutes away, I'm going to go there this afternoon."

Charlie lifts her brows. "Today?"

"Before I change my mind."

We sit in silence for a few minutes before

Charlie says, "You should tell Ava. She deserves to know."

A shiver races down my spine, because I know she's right. As much as I want to protect Ava from this, once the media gets ahold of the story, she'll be pulled into this.

I dial her number.

"Hey loser," Ava says when she answers.

"Is Prescott with you?"

"Um, yeah, why?"

I inhale a long, deep breath, then tell her, "Put me on speaker. He should know too."

Once I know that only they can hear our conversation, I tell them everything and my plan on visiting the Michaels. Prescott mutters a few explicit curses, but Ava remains silent.

"Need to do this," I say, emotion strangling me.

My sister says softly, "I know. You're doing the right thing."

But as I end the call, I'm not sure I am.

"You are," Charlie says as if reading my mind. She places a hand on my arm. "Doing the right thing."

"Will you come with me? I know it's a lot to ask, but—"

"Of course." Her fingers twine with mine, and I take the strength and support she offers freely.

I'm not sure I could do this without her. And later, when we pull into the driveway of the address Sam provided, it's Charlie who reminds me why I'm doing this.

"You're a good man, Spencer. You're not ruining the Beckett name. You're bringing honor to it."

"God, I love you." I kiss her hand, then get out of the car.

A woman in her mid to late fifties, tired and sad looking, opens the door as we approach. "Can I help you?"

Shit. I came all this way, and yet I have no fucking idea what I'm supposed to say.

"Mrs. Michaels?" Charlie asks when I hesitate, her fingers linked with mine.

"Yes." The woman nods, frowning.

"We wanted to talk to you about Shannon. Can we come in?"

Her eyes light up slightly. "You were friends with my girl? Of course." She opens the door wider so we can enter. "Please, come in. Make yourself at home." She takes our jackets and leads us to the living room, then offers, "Can I get you something to drink?"

"No," I say, finally finding my voice. I sit on the floral couch, Charlie beside me. "Is your husband here?"

"He's in the garage. I'll get him." She leaves us, and I sit there wondering how I'm just supposed to spit out the words.

"Just speak from your heart," Charlie whispers.

A few moments later, Mr. Michaels comes into the living room followed by his wife. He holds out a grease-stained hand I shake it.

"Anne says that you were friends with Shannon?"

"No, actually I never met your daughter." I drag my palms over my legs, feeling the weight of their frowns on me. "I came here, because..." God, this is hard. "I recently found out some information about her death."

Anne sits down in the chair across from me, her movement slow, her expression unreadable. Her husband puts a hand on her shoulder, which she takes, and they wait for me to continue.

"I remember hearing about the accident when it happened, but like I said, I didn't know her."

"If there's something you can tell us," the man,

whose name I know is John, chokes out, hope in his eyes. "Anything to help us...understand."

"I believe it was my brother who hit her."

Anne sucks in a shaky breath, but neither of them say anything, they just wait.

"I wasn't there, so I don't know what happened. I wish I could tell you more. But from what I know, he believed she died instantly. And he..." Emotions make it almost impossible to says the words. "He left her. I'm so sorry."

Silence. It stretches around us. Suffocating.

"Why are you telling us this?" John asks.

"I know I can't bring back your daughter. There's nothing I can say, or do, but I couldn't hide this..."

"And your brother, why isn't he here?" Anne asks, tears rolling over her cheeks.

"He took his own life, not long after."

Anne and John exchange looks, but I have no idea what they're thinking. I feel all the guilt, all the shame that should be Ethan's placed upon my shoulders.

"I'm so sorry." My voice cracks with the apology. I let out a shaky breath. "I'll make a statement to the police. And I'd like to start a scholarship fund in Shannon's name."

I'm not sure what I'm expecting. Threats. Screaming. Tears. But not what happens next. Both John and Anne move toward me. She wraps me in a hug, and he places a hand on my shoulder. I'm not sure how long they stay there, but it's long enough for tears to gather in my eyes.

"Thank you," Anne whispers before she pulls away.

"What's your name, son?" John asks.

"Spencer Beckett."

"You're a good man, Spencer. I know it wasn't easy for you coming here like this. But your brother's sins aren't your own. You don't have to carry the weight of it."

And for the first time since I found out what Ethan did, I feel that weight lifted. And it hits me, that next to love, maybe the second most powerful thing in this world, is forgiveness.

12

CHARLIE

THE MICHAELS ARE GOOD PEOPLE. I knew it when we walked in the door, but even I'm taken back by the acceptance they show Spencer. And it leaves my heart aching, because I wonder how things would have been different if Ethan had been brave enough to face his mistake, if it had been him in this room, confessing his transgressions. Maybe guilt wouldn't have killed him. Maybe he'd still be alive, and Spencer's family wouldn't be broken.

But he made his choice - the wrong one. And so did Spencer's dad. In the end, he may lose both of his sons because of it.

"Will you two stay for lunch?" Anne asks, wiping the tears from her cheeks. "Gavin is coming over with his wife and little boy. I'd like him to meet you."

"You have a son?" I ask as Spencer and John start their own conversation.

"Four," Anne says proudly. "Gavin is the oldest. Shannon was our...baby." She picks up a picture from the fireplace mantle and runs her hand over it longingly. "This was taken four Christmases ago. It was her last..."

I take the framed photo when she hands it to me. Their family is posed around a Christmas tree, all wearing matching Santa sweaters and making goofy faces.

"You have a beautiful family." I smile as I scan the happy faces and then freeze, my blood turning to ice when I recognize the youngest boy in the picture.

He's skinnier, and younger, with bleach blond highlights in his spiky hair, but it's him.

"Decan."

"You know Decan?" Anne asks, causing Spencer's gaze to jerk to mine.

"I uh..." My fingers tremble as I hand the photo to Spencer. "Yeah. Spencer and I go to Princeton."

Anne's eyes shine with pride. "He's on the football team. He got a scholarship. He's smart, just like Shannon was."

Confusion whips through me, a million pieces of a puzzle that fit together, even though I'm afraid of what the final picture will be.

Shannon was Decan's sister. It can't just be a coincidence. Can it?

I glance over at Spencer, and I can tell he's thinking the same thing.

But Winslow already admitted to creating the blogs and taking the photos. Was he working with her as some revenge plot to get back at the Becketts? But if he knew about Ethan, why hadn't he gone to the police or said anything?

There are more questions now than before.

"I actually have to get back to school," I say quickly, standing, then tell a small white lie, "I have class." I gather my things and tell Spencer, "I'll meet you in the car," before rushing out the door, needing fresh air.

I don't know if Decan is the person who has been making my life a living hell, but if he was - we might finally find some peace.

But as Spencer comes outside, unlocking the car - I see his eyes burning with anger.

I draw in a sharp breath. If I thought things

were about to get easier, I was wrong. Spencer's promise to protect me is one he won't back down on, even if I asked him to.

"I'll make this right," he says as we buckle ourselves into the car.

"It's like John said - you don't have to carry the weight of this." I don't want Spencer to fight my battles, because I can't bear the thought of something happening to him. Losing him. I love him too damn much.

But Spencer just pulls out of the driveway, reaching for my hand and squeezing it so tight it hurts. "I agree that my brother's sins aren't mine to carry - but making sure the person who has been threatening you pays for what they did when they ran you off the road - I'm carrying that. Not because I have to, Charlie. But because I want to."

13

SPENCER

"You can't go alone," Charlie says, her knees tucked under her chin as she sits on the couch.

We've been having the same argument for the last hour.

"I won't be alone. Prescott will be there."

"I just think we should wait. Maybe it's just a coincidence—"

"You know it's not. Think about it, Charlie. Take the blogs out of the equation. We know that was Winslow. But she wasn't the one who ran you off the road. And as sick and twisted as she is, the pig's blood isn't her style. Why would she go after Ava?"

"I don't know." She chews on her thumbnail. "I just think that you should let the police do their job.

If it was him, and he did somehow know that Ethan was responsible for killing Shannon, maybe once your statement is read, he'll be satisfied."

"You think I give a shit if he's satisfied? He almost killed you."

"But he didn't."

Frustrated, I drag my hands through my hair. "You admit it was him."

She shakes her head, but I see the truth in her eyes.

"I'm just going to talk to him." I lean down and cup her jaw. "That's all. Prescott will be there, and we'll meet in a public place. Nothing will happen."

"I just have a bad feeling about this."

I kiss her, feeling the same unease I see in her eyes. But the longer and harder I've thought about it, I know I'm right. Decan Michaels may not have been Charlie's stalker, but I have no doubt that he was the one who forced her off the road that night.

I remember his parents' arms around me, their forgiveness. And I want to be that man. But I also need to make sure that Charlie is safe, first and always.

"Not sure why we're doing this here," Prescott says, leaning back in his chair, eyes scanning the crowded coffee shop. "If it were up to me, we'd be having this conversation in the back alley."

I grunt. "Which is why it isn't up to you. And this place doesn't even have a back alley."

Prescott shrugs, then I see his expression change. "The asshole is here."

"Remember, let me do the talking."

Decan walks into the coffee shop, his gaze jerky until it lands on me. His lips twist in a scowl before he pushes his way through the line of people and takes a seat across from me.

We study each other for a few moments before Prescott breaks the silence, "Time to fess up, jackass. We know you're the one who ran Charlie off the road."

I have to hold back an eye roll, Prescott has never followed orders.

"You always need a wingman, Beckett?" Decan says. "First, Tatum, now this douche. Can't fight your battles yourself?" He scoffs. "You're as much of a coward as your brother."

"So you knew." I keep my voice calm, low. I'm not here to fight. I'm here to make sure he never goes near Charlie or Ava again.

"That your brother killed my sister? Yeah, I knew. Not that the police believed me. Or if they did, your father paid them off. Even my parents thought I made it up. She called me, did you know that?" He laughs, but it's a bitter sound, full of rage. "No, you wouldn't. Because it wasn't on the police report. They even managed to delete the phone records. It just goes to show, that money can buy anything, even a man's innocence."

"What do you mean, she called you?" I ask, my throat falling into my stomach, not sure I want to hear his answer. "I saw the medical report, she died instantly."

There are tears in his eyes when he says, "She wasn't dead. Not right away. But your brother, he left her there. Bleeding. In pain. She called me. Begged me to help her. And she told me..." His left eye twitches. "She told me that your brother had stood over her as she pleaded for him to help her, before taking off. He didn't even call an ambulance. She could have...could have lived. But instead, she bled out, on the cold road, alone."

"Fuck," Prescott mutters.

I feel it too. And I get the man's anger, his feeling of injustice. Even his need for revenge.

"I'm sorry, about Shannon—"

"You don't get to say her name," Decan spits out. "You might have my parents fooled with your little sorry-act, but I know you. You Becketts are all the same. You knew I was getting closer to the truth. That's why—"

"You're wrong. I didn't know. Not until recently. And I want to make things right. But what you did, hurting Charlie—"

"I didn't fucking know she was driving the car," he spits out. "I thought it was you."

It's an admittance of guilt. But I'm not sure what to do with it.

"And the dorm rooms? The pig's blood? That was you?"

He sneers, and even though he doesn't acknowledge it, I see the truth in his eyes.

I want to kick his ass, but it'll get us nowhere.

"Here's what we're going to do," I say, steadily, placing my forearms on the table. "No more people get hurt. We expose the truth. For Shannon, for your parents. The whole truth. Including your part in it. The car accident, the vandalism. It's over, Decan."

His eyes narrow. "Over? You think this will ever be over? Your family took something from me, and I won't stop until I take something from you."

He stands and starts to walk away, but I move quickly, blocking him.

But it's Prescott that grabs him, shoving him backward. "You go near, Ava—"

"Or what?" Decan spits out, something feral in his eyes. I hear the click of metal before I see the gun. Decan raises it and points it straight at Prescott's chest.

It takes less than a second before the entire coffee shop is in chaos. People scream, chairs are being pushed back, coffees are spilled as the crowd tries to move toward the doors.

"You going to shoot me?" Prescott scoffs. "You don't have the balls. But I can guarantee that you're going to rot in jail after this."

I want to smack Prescott for egging him on, because Decan looks completely unhinged at the moment, and the gun he's holding isn't a toy.

"You don't want him," I say, keeping my hands up as Decan points the gun at me. "Your fight is with me. Right?" I take a step closer and meet his eyes. "You want me to suffer for what my brother did? I get it. I felt the same way when Charlie was in the hospital. Wanted whoever had done it to her to pay."

"It's not the same."

"No, you're right. It's not. Because I'm not the person who took your sister from you. But you are the one who almost took Charlie from me."

"I didn't know it was her." His hands shake as he continues to point the gun at my chest.

"Right. You thought it was me. And if you'd killed me? If you kill me now. You think that'll fix things? You think Shannon will be proud of her big brother?"

"Shut up." He jams one palm into his temple, still holding the gun at me. "Shut up, shut up."

"Put the gun down, Decan." There are sirens in the distance. "The cops are already on their way. This isn't going to end well."

"But at least it will end." His eyes are glossy, vacant, and I know he came here with every intention of killing me.

Prescott moves, and when he does, Decan points the gun at him, and as if in slow motion, I see his finger pull back on the trigger. I don't think, I just react. I lunge at him as the gun goes off.

Glass shatters and there's more screaming. And then I'm being yanked backward, my hands being cuffed behind me. And two men in uniforms are on Decan, and the gun is taken from his hand.

Chaos rages around me. Prescott is screaming at

someone, but as far as I can tell he isn't hurt. I don't care that I'm being pushed into the police car, don't care that this day is going to be a long one to get through. I can see the reports and statements that will be required of Prescott and me before we get cleared to go.

But I don't care. Not about any of that.

I care that no one was hurt. That Decan is no longer holding a gun, pointing it at me, at Prescott, at himself.

Hours later, as the police car pulls away from the dramatic scene at the coffee shop, I stare at the chaos, at the shattered window.

A million shards of glass, each one capable of causing deep wounds, cuts that kill. Or they can be melted together and forged into a new piece of glass, something beautiful.

I wish Ethan would have taken his horrific mistake and redeemed himself. That he would have let himself be forged by the fire and come out whole.

But he's gone, and Shannon is gone.

And nothing can change that.

The only thing we can do is learn from it.

I've struggled for so long, trying to figure out what kind of man I want to be. Hating the money, the power - but I don't need to fight it anymore. I can choose what I want to do with the life I've been granted. And I want to do good. I want to fight for justice. For the right thing even when it's hard, even when it's scary. Even when it puts me in a vulnerable place.

Shannon's parents taught me that forgiveness is a fucking powerful tool. When you aren't able to let go, you turn into a man like Decan, burning with hate. That won't be my story. Not now, not ever.

There are no guarantees in the path less taken, but fortune favors the brave.

14

CHARLIE

"The media is relentless," Spencer says, rolling over in bed, his phone in hand. He's been up for hours, scrolling through articles that are rehashing the Beckett Family Scandal. So many of them feature images of Spencer being handcuffed, pushed into a police car. Other articles focus on Ethan and Geoffrey, calling them monsters. Declaring their misuse of money and power being the essential problem with our judicial system.

None of it is good.

"Stop looking at it, it's going to make you crazy," I tell him, turning to face him.

"Too late." He sighs, dropping his phone on the sheets. "I hate all of this."

"You did the right thing." I run my hand

over his bare chest, firm muscles tighten beneath my fingers. He's been going on long runs every day, spending hours at the gym. He says it's the one thing right now that clears his mind - and I'm glad he has some sort of release.

"I just hate that the right thing feels so fucking wrong."

"Your parents didn't call?" I had my final shift at work last night and got home late after he was already in bed.

"No, they spoke with Ava though. Apparently I'm being written out of the will."

"That's…"

"Pointless?" Spencer may say it's pointless, but I can tell he is rattled by it. "I have a trust they can't touch. I was already given the Nantucket house, and you own this one. They can't hurt me by taking away money I'd inherit when they're dead. It's petty."

"I know," I say, trying to put myself in his shoes. "Are you sure you want to go to this event tonight? With everything going on—"

"It's exactly why we should go. I'm not going to hide because of what my father and Ethan did." He pulls me to him, a smile tugging at his lips. "Plus, it's a ball. I think it's only fitting that Prince Charming and Cinderella show up."

I wrap my arms around his neck and kiss the tip of his nose. "Jill and Daphne are pretty excited. Daphne is letting me borrow this gorgeous dress—"

"I wish you would have let me buy you a new one."

"Why? It's not like I'll ever have anywhere to wear it again. Just seems like a waste of money. Especially now that you're going to have to scrimp and save like the rest of us."

He grunts. "Hardly."

I give him another kiss before getting out of bed. "I know how to cut coupons, hunt for bargains at the thrift store." I pull on my bathrobe. "You're lucky to have me."

He smiles, his face relaxing for the first time in days. "We could skip the Princeton Ball and—"

I shake my head and cut him off. "Nope. You are going for a run. Showering. And then you are picking me up at eight."

"God I love it when you're bossy," he says, grabbing my waist and kissing my belly. His hand slides under my robe and he teases my nipples with his fingers.

I swat his hand away playfully. "You want some of that? Then you need to be wearing a tux."

"Is that a promise?" he asks.

I shake my head. "No, Princeton Charming, that's a guarantee."

"So this is how the one percent live," Jill says taking in the luxury apartment. Daphne, Georgie, and I follow her as a maid lets us in. "It's so gorgeous."

The Becketts bought it for Ava after the vandalism at the dorm. They may not have been here physically to support her after the incident, but this apartment at least gives Ava the sense of security she needs.

"If you want to stay here this summer you totally can, Jill," Ava says leading us to her bedroom. "I'm going to be in Australia after school gets out and then I'll be in London for ten weeks."

"I would never want to impose."

Daphne tsks. "But Jill, you'll be in Princeton all summer working. Don't the dorms close?"

"For a few weeks. I figured I'd find an Air BnB."

"You're not doing that," Ava says. "I insist. And

Harriet comes three times a week to clean. It would be rude to not give her something to do."

Jill and I share a look. I shrug. "They're right. I just feel like a jerk for not thinking of it myself. Our place will be empty too."

"You are both way too generous."

Ava smiles widely at Jill before she pushes open the double French doors that lead to her suite. "Then it's settled."

"Holy smokes," I say taking in the scene before me. There are five chairs positioned in front of full-length mirrors, racks of designer gowns, cases of glittering jewels. Two makeup artists stand with brushes ready, and two hair stylists are plugging in curling irons.

"What do you think?" Ava squeals, clapping her hands. "Here, ladies, read this," she says, handing me a card as Harriet offers us each a mimosa.

Dear Ava, Daphne, Georgie, Jill, and Charlie,
You all deserve to look like royalty tonight.
Treat yourselves like the Princesses you are.
The limo will be here at eight o'clock.

. . .

Your Charming Dates,
   Prescott, Tatum, Yates, Connery, and Spencer

"I still can't believe Tatum is taking me," Daphne says. "It was really sweet of him."

I smile, having asked Tatum myself if he might take Daphne to the ball. There is no chemistry between the two, and they are hardly friends, but I knew it would mean a lot for her. Tatum agreed with a smile, telling me he wasn't seeing anyone and would be happy to take her.

The fact that he followed through - and is now doing this for us girls, with the Princeton Elite - tells me everything anyone needs to know about Tatum.

"This was so sweet," Jill says. "I mean Connery is seriously winning points tonight."

"You two keeping score?" Georgia asks.

Jill laughs. "I don't know what we are, but every time we hang out, I laugh until I cry."

"Has he kissed you?" Georgie presses and I realize she is very invested in this situation. She is with Yates, and Connery and he are two peas in a pod.

"Not yet," Jill says. "But if he doesn't make a move tonight I'll make one for him."

We all crack, and that is the Jill I know and love.

"All of this arrived this morning," Ava explains. "I was planning on wearing that Vera dress from last year's fashion week. Remember, the blue lace?" she asks Daphne who nods, hanging onto every word. "Anyway, then this all came right after I got out of the shower and I mean, look, it's all this year's pieces. The boys must have paid a fortune."

"And we're here to help," one of the hairdressers says as they come over to us and introduce themselves. "My name is Gizel and we will help make all your dreams come true," the stunning woman says with a smile. If she's doing my makeup tonight, I trust her implicitly. Her skin is glowing, and her hair is shiny. She looks like magic. "Now, who is ready to try on some dresses?"

Our mimosas are topped off and we begin looking through the racks, holding up options, asking one another for opinions. My mother would have loved hearing about this. I remember how one of the last things we did together was put together my New Year's Eve dress. We changed the hemline and took it in a bit. It was so sweet, her excitement for me to go with Spencer on a whirlwind date in Manhattan.

Tears prick my eyes thinking of how many

things I wish I could share with her now. She would have never left my side when I was in the hospital after the accident. She would have sent me boxes of her famous peanut butter cookies congratulating me for taking down the blogger who turned out to be Winslow. She would have called, listened to me cry over the phone as I told her about Decan's sister, about Ethan's part in that loss.

"You okay?" Ava asks, resting a hand on my arm.

I blink back tears. "It's been a big year," I tell her. "But I'm really glad that you've been a part of it, Ava." I pull her into a hug. I'm not really a touchy-feely person, but she feels like family. Like the sister I never had. And I hold her now, feeling so damn grateful to have her in my life.

"Sweetie, me too." Ava pulls back, wiping her own eyes. "Remember when you found me in the grass? Drunk and such a mess? You saved my life."

"Spencer was so mad," I say, remembering that night. "I had no idea that your brother would be walking into the hospital and that months later we'd be in love."

"You guys are so sweet it makes my teeth hurt," she laughs. "Now tell, what dress did you choose?"

I twist my lips, looking around. Then I see it.

The only one that I'd consider. Walking toward it, Ava is beside herself. Truthfully, so am I,

"I think he chose it for me himself, don't you?" I ask, taking in the blue gown with the full skirt.

Ava looks at the inside. "Yeah, it was handmade, not a label in sight. Oh look, there is a tag."

I pull out the card that is pinned to the inside. It reads, *For my Cinderella. Love, your Princeton Charming.*

"Oh my gosh, this dress was definitely made for you, Charlotte Hayes."

I hold it up to myself. It will fit like a glove.

BY THE TIME we are dressed and ready to go it's just after seven. Daphne chose a bright pink structured gown by Zac Posen. Ava went for an edgier, strapless Badgley Mischka in nude, covered with oversized rhinestones. Georgie, ever the classic beauty, opted for a plunging red Burberry dress. And Jill went for a vintage black Dior that hugs her curves so perfectly it even gets me a little hot and bothered. If that doesn't get Connery to make a move, I don't know what will.

Harriet has set out a spread of appetizers, but

we are all too nervous to eat. Except Daphne. She's suddenly got a crazy appetite.

"Slow down, chicka," I say catching the cracker and brie as it almost lands on her exquisite dress. She's eating so fast she dropped her food. "What's up?"

"I just have a lot on my mind, Charlie. *A lot.*" Daphne is always dramatic and I'm assuming going with Tatum has her spun up.

"Like what?"

"I can't really talk to you about it. I mean, not now."

"Okay, later then?"

She nods, picking up a bacon covered date. "Later."

I squeeze her arm, then go back to Ava's bedroom to grab my handbag. Gizel, the elegant woman who did my makeup is putting her things away.

"Did you need a touch-up?" she asks.

I look at myself in the mirror. The dress Spencer had made for me is so dreamy, with layers upon layers of gossamer fabric, tiny crystals sewn into the bodice. It's off the shoulder with delicate tulle.

"What do you think?"

Gizel assesses me. "Well you didn't put on any jewelry," she comments.

"I thought the crystals on the dress were enough."

Gizel shakes her head, laughing. "No such thing as too much. Here, I know what you need."

She pulls out a tiara from one of the cases.

"I think it might be over the top," I say.

But she isn't having any of it. "Just try, Princess."

She places it on my head, and when she does, I have to admit, it finishes the look. I'm not usually the kind of girl who gets all fluttery over pretty things, but right now, I feel so beautiful.

Jill, Ava, Daphne, and Georgie come in the room, grabbing their bags, announcing that the guys are here.

They pause when they see me.

"Oh Charlie, it's perfect," Georgie says, her voice hushed and so sincere it makes my heart ache in a good way.

"You sure? Spencer won't think I went overboard?"

Ava laughs. "He's the one who bought you the dress."

"And after the year you've had, sweetie," Jill says. "You get anything you want."

"Your dates have arrived, ladies," Harriet says.

Everyone giggles with excitement and it's like we're all headed to our senior prom all over again.

I give Gizel a hug before I leave. "Thanks for being my Fairy Godmother tonight."

15

SPENCER

When Charlie and I walk into the ballroom, everyone turns. I know why. She looks so beautiful tonight. She always does - but this is different. This is magic. We didn't arrive in a carriage, but damn, this woman is my fucking fairy tale.

"Everyone is staring," she murmurs, holding onto my arm.

"Let them." I chuckle. "It's good for everyone to know you're mine."

"I am." Her smile is bright with the truth of it.

The Princeton ballroom has been turned into a glittering, magical place. There are a thousand twinkling lights hung from the ceilings, live trees and flowers have been brought in, making it an indoor garden. There's a band on stage and servers walk around with trays of champagne.

"Want one?" Charlie asks, taking a flute of bubbly.

"Yeah, so long as you don't toss it in my face," I tease.

The ball is for the senior class. I came two years ago, but it was nothing like this. Mostly because Charlie wasn't my date. With her by my side, everything is better. Even the fall-out with my parents seems inconsequential knowing I have her.

"I sent my dad some photos of us," she says as we walk through the room with our champagne, taking a moment to talk alone.

"I bet he loved seeing you all dressed up."

She nods. "I miss him. But he'll be here in a few months for graduation."

"We should have him come with us to Nantucket for a week or two."

Charlie squeezes my arm, looking up at me and I know I made the right suggestion. "Really?"

"Of course, he deserves a vacation more than any man I know." And he does. After the year he's had, losing his business and much more importantly, his wife, Daniel deserves all the blessings in the world. "Do you think he'd ever consider moving to the East Coast?"

"I don't know," she says. "He's living with family now, working at his brother's shop. I'm not sure what he wants."

"Ask him."

She smiles, kissing my cheek. "I will."

"Now," I say, depositing our glasses on a passing tray. "Can I have the next dance?"

She presses a hand to her heart. "I was wondering when you'd ask."

The music slows the moment we reach the dance floor, and I pull her to me, a hand on her waist, holding onto the woman I love.

She looks longingly into my eyes as we move around the dance floor. It feels like we are the only two people in the world, even though there are hundreds of people around us. When she is in my arms, everything else fades away.

I kiss her as the song ends, holding onto her, her lips pressed against mine. I feel her heat, her longing, her love.

We pull back from the kiss, and I ask, "What was it you said about me wearing a tux?"

She lifts her eyebrows. "You sure you can handle it?"

"You doubt me?"

She shakes her head. "Not for a second." Then she takes my hand.

"Where are we going?"

"You'll see."

At the coat check, she asks for Tanya. I frown, not knowing her. "Hey," Charlie says. "The key?"

Tanya smiles. "Right." She produces a keyring from her pocket. "Have fun."

"What was that?" I ask, following Charlie down the hall, her beautiful blue dress swishing as she walks.

"You're not the only one with connections, you know. Yours just happen to be in high places, mine in low ones." She stops at a door labeled Storage. "I've been working on campus since freshman year, I've scouted out the good places to have a quickie."

I laugh. "And the storage closet is one of them?"

She pushes open the door and drags me in. "Yes, Spencer Beckett, it is." Her fingers spin the lock, and she pulls me to her. "Fuck me against the door, Prince Charming."

My eyes widen and my cock grows stiff at her words. "Filthy Princess," I say, a hand on her waist, my other on her face, tilting her chin up so she can look me in the eyes. More than ready to ravish her. "I think I need to clean you up."

"I don't want to be clean," she teases, her hand on my belt, undoing it and tugging my cock free. "I want to be dirty."

I pull up the skirt of her dress and raise a brow. "No panties?"

She shakes her head, grinning. "I had plans for this."

"Good girl." I cup her ass, my fingers finding her slit, she's wet and ready, but I'm going to make my lover beg. I lift her leg, her back against the door, and I finger her gently. Teasing her clit with tight circles, showing her how capable I am of making all her dreams come true.

"Play nice," she whimpers as I press a finger in and out, her pussy both excited and desperate.

"I'll tell you when to come, understood?"

She nods as I move my hand faster, faster, taking her so close to the edge I know she's ready to scream, to cry out my name. Good.

I pull back my hand, draw my finger to my mouth, and suck her creamy release off my finger. "Fuck, you taste good."

She's whimpering against the door, her hand

moving toward her pussy. "I can't wait," she tells me. "I need to come."

I lift my girl up, layers of organza and lace between us, and I set her down on my cock. "There you go, right where you belong."

She closes her eyes as I take her, as I fill her tight little pussy up the way we both need.

"This is where you can come. On my cock, you understand?"

She opens her eyes, wrapping her hands around my neck. "I like it when you talk dirty too," she pants as I thrust inside her needy warmth.

"And I like it when I get you off."

"Oh Spencer," she cries, so close to the edge. "Spencer, I love you, I love you, so much," she whispers, her breath ragged and her need so damn clear. Need for me. For us.

"God, I love you too," I say, thrusting again as my raging cock brings her where she is so damn desperate to go.

She comes, her walls tightening as my throbbing length fills her up with hot come. She clings to me as I kiss her. Inhaling her, holding on to the woman I love and refusing to let go. Ever. God, I need her now and forever.

"Spencer," she gasps, our foreheads touching as

we finish. As our bodies hum with life and passion and need for one another.

I hold her against me, not wanting to let go. Our eyes lock and I know this story won't end at midnight. Charlie is going to be mine, for as long as we both shall live.

16

CHARLIE

Leaving the storage room and reentering the ballroom, Spencer and I are in a cocoon of love and lust and so much passion I don't trust myself not to have my way with him right here on the dance floor.

"You okay?" he asks, our fingers laced together.

"I'm about thirty minutes from leaving this party and having round two back at our place."

Spencer grins, kissing me again. I know he's still hard for me, and God, my pussy is so wet for him.

"I need to go outside and get some air," he says chuckling.

"I bet you do," I say laughing, trying not to look at his groin. "I'll go find the girls."

He kisses me on the cheek, telling me he'll be

back soon and I go off, looking for the ladies I came here with.

I find Daphne as she is leaving the bar and I wave her down. She's clearly stumbling in her heels and when she says hello, her words slur.

"You might want to slow down on those." I frown at Daphne who is double fisting two glasses of champagne.

She was already acting off earlier today, and the alcohol isn't making things any better.

"I'm fine," she mumbles, draining one glass and handing it to a man who walks by with his date, clearly mistaking him for a server.

Across the room Spencer glances away from the conversation he's having with Prescott and Yates and smiles at me, making me forget for a moment why I came over here - to rescue Daphne from herself.

When she sways, I take her elbow and lead her into another room, finding her a bench to sit down on.

"Just take a break, okay?" I try to take the glass of champagne from her, but she drinks it before I can.

"I'm having fun...I'm allowed to have fun." Tears well in her eyes and her gaze goes distant, her words so slurred I wonder if she even knows what she's saying. "I thought I'd feel better…"

I sigh. "You'll feel better once you sleep this off. Let me call you an Uber."

"No." She lies down on the bench and pulls her gown around her like a blanket. "I just need a small rest."

People walk by and I hear the whispers and giggles.

"What's going on?" Jill says, coming up beside me and frowning at Daphne.

"Charlotte's being a party pooper," Daphne mutters. "Oh God, I shouldn't have eaten those hor d'oeuvres."

Jill helps her sit up. "Maybe we should take you to the restroom."

Daphne shakes her head. "I just…need another drink…need to stop seeing it…always seeing her…"

"I'll call her a ride," I tell Jill. "I'll take her home."

"No." Daphne stands, wobbling when she does and doing a poor job at fixing her updo that's hanging haphazardly around her face. She points a finger at me, stumbling. "Perfect princess Charlotte. You can't tell me what to do."

"I'm just trying to help."

She laughs. "I wanted to help you. I tried to warn you about Beckett..."

Jill has to catch her from falling forward. "Spencer's a good guy. He's proven himself."

"Ethan was a bad, bad guy..." Daphne sits back down, her eyes closing. "I thought...thought he loved me..."

Both Jill and I look at each other and frown.

"You knew Ethan?" I ask, but Daphne seems to have passed out now.

"I don't think she knows what she's saying," Jill says. "But you shouldn't have to miss out on tonight. Go dance with your boyfriend, have your Cinderella moment, I'll take care of her."

"You're sure?" I glance down at Daphne, her lipstick and mascara is smeared across her face now.

"I'm good. This isn't really my scene anyway. And I already got what I came for." She winks and I know that she and Connery must have finally kissed. "I was going to sneak out in a bit anyway."

"Alone?" I raise my brows at her, and her cheeks turn a shade of red.

"Don't make a big deal about it or I might chicken out."

I make a motion like I'm zipping my lips, but I can't help the smile that makes my face hurt.

Jill stays with Daphne as I go back into the ballroom, looking for Spencer and Connery to help us get Daphne in the car.

"Daphne looks wasted," Prescott says when he sees me.

"Jill's taking her home," I tell him. "Would you mind helping her. I can't find Spencer."

"Yeah, sure."

"Thanks." Things between Prescott and I are better now. I don't know if it's all because of Ava, but he's not the same asshole he was when I first met him.

"Hey, Charlotte." Tatum approaches me as Prescott walks away. He rubs the back of his neck and gives me a crooked smile. "I was wondering if you wanted to dance? That's if your boyfriend doesn't mind." He nods and I follow his gaze across the room where Spencer is talking to Yates and Georgia.

"Sure." I take Tatum's arm and he leads me onto the dance floor.

He's a bit clumsy, his large body meant for playing football, not ballroom dancing, but I can tell he asked me not to show off his dance moves, but to talk. There are still things between us, wounds that may never heal. And I know I hurt him more than once.

"How have you been?" we ask at the same time.

I laugh. "I'm good. Better now that we know who was creating the blogs, and who ran me off the road."

"Yeah. I'm glad Decan's behind bars. Wish Winslow was there too for what she did to you."

"I don't think she'll be a problem anymore."

"That's good." He moves me around the dance floor, a frown tugging at his lips. "I want you to be happy, Charlotte. I wish I could say that's all I ever wanted, but you know that's not true. I'll always...care about you."

"I know. And I am happy. I know you and Spencer haven't always gotten along—"

Tatum grunts. "That's the understatement of the year. But I can see how much he loves you and for that, I can respect him. But if he ever hurts you..."

I chuckle. "I know you've got my back."

"So we're good?"

"Yeah, Tatum, we're good."

He gives a hard nod as the song ends, then leans over and kisses my cheek, before turning and walking away.

It's weird, but as I watch him, I feel like it's

some kind of ending. And maybe it is. Tatum will always hold a special place in my heart, but things between us have changed.

I frown when I see Jill walking toward me, her eyes filled with worry, lips thin.

"Did you see her? Daphne?" Jill glances around the room and shakes her head. "I was talking to Prescott. We had our backs turned for just a second and she disappeared."

"Did you check the restrooms?" I follow Jill back out into the lobby.

"Yeah, she's not there."

"She's not outside, either," Prescott says as he approaches. "Maybe she got a car herself and left."

"Maybe," I mumble. But something doesn't feel right. And if the last few months has taught me anything, it's to trust my gut. I'm going to find her.

17

SPENCER

"Shit," Yates says. "Don't look now, but trouble is coming."

I wince when I see Winslow walking toward us. She smiles at Yates and Georgia, but neither of them return it. She's burned too many bridges, and she won't find any friendly faces here.

"Spencer, I was hoping..." She's flustered, and her usual confidence is gone. "Can I speak to you alone?"

I glance at Yates and Georgia and nod. They both frown at Winslow before walking away.

"What do you want?"

"To apologize."

I grunt and take a sip of my scotch. "You're

apologizing to the wrong person. It's Charlie you owe—"

"I know. But I don't think she's willing to talk to me. If you could tell her...I was a bitch."

"You were worse than that. You did real damage."

"There's no excuse for what I did, but I was grieving. I loved you, and Ethan..." She sniffs. "When I heard on the news what he did. God, I can't believe he kept that from all of us. No wonder he was such a mess."

"Ethan dug his own grave." The words might be callous, but it's how I feel right now. "But that's what happens when you let sin fester. It eats at you until you're nothing but the guilt and shame inside you. That's what drove him off that cliff."

"I thought..." She chews on her bottom lip, her eyes going distant for a moment. "After the accident, I thought for the longest time that it was my fault somehow. I saw the darkness in him, the way he used drugs to try and fill the emptiness. I wanted...I tried, to be the person he needed. But I couldn't..."

"His death wasn't on you." I understand the guilt she felt, I'd believed it myself. Thought if I'd only been a better brother, if I'd pushed him to get help, that maybe he'd still be alive today. "Ethan made his choice."

She nods, then dabs her fingers under her eyes. "I guess we're all responsible for our own choices."

"We are," I say, my voice hard.

"I know you'll never forgive me."

"No. That's where you're wrong, Winslow. I forgive you." The Michaels taught me that important lesson. Decan's lack of, and his parents' complete forgiveness. One destroyed while the other healed.

"Really?" There's hope in her eyes, and she starts to move toward me. "Spencer, I promise—"

I hold my hand out, stopping her. "I forgive you. But I'll never trust you again. This is our last conversation. I don't want you anywhere near me or Charlie. If there are family get-togethers, you don't go. Do you understand?"

She sucks in a shaky breath. "Yes."

"Goodbye, Winslow," I say before turning on my heels and walking away.

I hear her soft sob behind me, and maybe at one time it might have pulled at my emotions, but now I feel nothing for the woman who had been my first everything. Now I scan the room for the woman who will be my last, my future, my tomorrows.

She'd been dancing with Tatum, but she's no longer on the dance floor, and when I hear a commotion in the lobby, I feel a tickle of premonition at the nape of my neck.

"What?" I ask Prescott as he walks toward me, frowning.

"We've got a situation," he says. "It's Daphne. She's drunk out of her mind. And we can't find her."

"Just tell me Charlie is safe."

"Yeah, she's right there—" He stops when he looks over his shoulder. "Shit, she was..."

The pressure builds in my skull, and I try to stop the anxiety that builds in my chest. Everything is fine. Daphne is just drunk. Winslow has been put in her place, and Decan can't hurt her anymore.

But then I hear the shouting, and I know I was right. "There's someone on the roof and they're going to jump."

18

CHARLIE

As soon as I hear the people screaming, I know it's Daphne on the roof. I don't think, I just take off, rolling my ankle as I push through the crowd and find the stairwell, taking two steps at a time. I'm out of breath by the time I reach the fifth floor and push through the heavy metal door that leads to the roof.

For a heart-stopping moment, I don't see her, and I fear that I'm too late. That she's already jumped.

Oh god, no.

But then I hear a small sob. Off to my left, Daphne is standing on the ledge of the roof, her heels are off and her gown whips around in the wind. The stars are out, and it should be a magical spring night - not this. Not Daphne taking her own life.

I want to scream, to run up to her and drag her off the ledge, but I know any sudden movement could have her falling forward.

When she staggers slightly, I suck in a breath.

"Daphne," I say softly, moving slowly toward her.

She glances over her shoulder at me, black lines of mascara streaking her cheeks. "You can't stop me...it's too late..."

"I don't know what's going on, but we can fix things. Whatever it is. Let me help you."

She shakes her head violently, and almost loses her balance. "They...they said that she was still alive..."

"Who?" I take another step closer.

"The girl. On the news. They said she was alive. He told me...he said..." A gut-wrenching sob rips from her chest. "He said she was dead. And we just left her..."

Ice fills my veins. "Daphne. What are you talking about?"

Her words are mixed with her sobs and I can barely understand her words. "He said he loved me. He..." She hiccups. "He was my first."

"Who?" I ask, even though I'm pretty sure I know the answer.

"Ethan. He was so...handsome. Remember how I told you I lost someone freshman year?"

My heart pounds as pieces come together in my mind. "Were you...were you in the car when he hit Shannon?"

Her expression changes. It's like all her emotions have been ripped from her, and the girl who stares back at me is void, numb, empty. When she speaks again, her words are monotone. "He said he'd ruin me if I told anyone. He would have. And I thought...I didn't know the girl was still alive when we left. I would have called an ambulance... would have stayed." She staggers slightly, and I hear the gasps and cries of people below. "I killed her."

"No." I take another step toward her. "You didn't. Ethan did."

She shakes her head. "I can't live with it...not anymore. I see her body lying on that road...I called Ethan after, but he threatened me..."

"You sent Spencer the recording?"

"I wanted him to know. Wanted everyone to know. But I was too afraid. Even after he died, I didn't know if the Becketts would come after me. No one would believe..."

"It's okay." I'm close to her now, almost close enough to grab her hand and pull her back. "We'll figure it out."

She turns away and I see her start to take a step off the ledge.

"Daphne," I scream as I reach for her, my fingers grasping material. She falls back toward me, her limbs hitting at me wildly, pushing me away, and then I'm falling.

My bare arms scrape on stone and cement as I tumble over. My gown catches on something and I hear the material rip as I grasp for something, anything to stop my fall.

People yell and cry below me.

"Charlotte," Daphne shouts above me, her arm extended to me. "Take my hand."

My fingers slip slightly on the ledge I'm holding onto, and even if I could reach her, I know neither of us has the strength to pull me up.

I was a fool to think we'd all find our happily-ever-after. I'm hanging on for dear life, my eyes filling with tears as my fingers slip.

This isn't how the fairy tale was supposed to end.

19

SPENCER

As I burst through the steel door at the top of the building, I watch Charlie fall over the edge of the roof and it's like it's happening in slow motion. She screams and so do I as I race to the ledge, knowing I'll never make it in time.

By some miracle, Charlie is hanging onto a ledge, but she's too far down for me to reach her.

"Just hold on," I yell, not knowing what to do.

"Spencer," Charlie cries. "I can't...Oh, god...Please..."

"I'll get you, just don't let go." I have no idea where Prescott ran off to.

"She's going to die!" Daphne sobs and every fiber in my being refuses to believe it.

No. Not the woman I love. Not now, after everything we've been through.

I pull my jacket off, ready to climb over the ledge myself. It's not a great plan, but I don't know what else to do.

"What are you doing?" Daphne gasps as I swing one leg over the ledge.

"Spencer, no..." Charlie cries out.

A huge crowd has formed below us, and I can hear sirens in the distance. Already a cop car is pulling up to the curb. They'll be here in minutes, but Charlie's fingers keep slipping and I know she doesn't have minutes.

"I'm going to try and grab your arm," I tell her.

"You'll fall." Charlie's eyes are wide with fear.

We're four stories up. And when one of her shoes falls off, bouncing off the stone masonry that juts out of the building and landing on the hard cement below, a vision of Charlie's body doing the same slams into me.

Fuck.

Straddling the ledge, I hold on with one hand and reach for Charlie with the other. My fingers brush hers, but I'm still too high to reach her.

Tears streak her cheeks. "Spencer."

The police are out of their cars now, probably

inside the building, but Charlie's fingers keep slipping. She's barely hanging on by the tips of them, and there's blood around her nails from digging into the stone.

"I can't hold on..."

A window smashes below me, and I see Prescott below using his jacket to push away the jagged edges. He's only a couple feet from her.

"I've got you," he says, stepping out onto the ledge, and wrapping an arm around her waist. "Let go."

Charlie whimpers looking up at me before releasing her grip and wrapping her arms around Prescott's neck.

I don't think I take a real breath until Prescott is helping her through the broken window. Cheers below float up, and as grateful as I am that Charlie is safe, anger seizes me as I glance over at Daphne, who has sunken into an emotional heap of tulle and tears.

"What the hell were you thinking?" I growl out, grabbing her arm and pulling her up and away from the ledge so that she can't try anything stupid again.

"I'm sor-sorry...I didn't mean...never meant to hurt anyone..."

I know I should feel some sympathy for the girl, she was up here wanting to end her life, but the fact that she put Charlie in danger has the Neanderthal in me beating my chest.

"Just want it all to end."

"For fuck's sake, Daphne. You think anything ends when a person kills them self? They just make life a living hell for the people they leave behind."

The roof door opens, and two police officers come through, followed by Prescott and Charlie.

I let the police deal with the still sobbing Daphne and open my arms to Charlie who falls into them. "Can you please stop fucking scaring me like that."

She sucks in a shaky breath, trembling against me. "I had to stop her."

"I know." I press my lips to the top of her head and glance over at Prescott. There's blood on his arms and hands from the window, and he looks almost as shaken up as I feel. "Thank you."

He gives a hard nod. I know I owe him more than a thanks, but right now all I can do is hold Charlie and breathe her in. I used to be a thrill seeker, wanting the next adrenaline high, but I'll be happy to sit in a padded room for the rest of my life if it means never feeling like this again.

The cops are talking to Daphne, and Prescott goes over to them.

"She was in the car," Charlie says, her words muffled against my chest.

"What?" I place my palm on her cheek and lift her face so I can see her eyes. And my heart stutters as I meet her gaze. God, I love her so damn much. The thought of ever losing her guts me.

"Daphne. She was with Ethan that night. She was in the car when he hit Shannon."

I shake my head, trying to process her words. I didn't even know they knew each other.

"She was the one who sent you the recording of Ethan confessing. He was talking to her."

"Shit." I pull Charlie closer and glance over at Daphne. Paramedics are with her now. I hadn't even seen them arrive.

"They're taking her to the hospital," Prescott says, approaching. "Pretty sure the police want to talk to you both." He places a hand on Charlie's shoulder. "You okay?"

She nods and hesitates before hugging Prescott. "Thank you. You were really brave. You saved my life and I won't forget that."

He actually blushes. "Yeah…" He rubs the back of his neck. "Well, all things considered, I guess you aren't so bad, Hayes. In fact, I'm kind of getting used to having you around. Just try not to go jumping off of a building again."

She gives him a small smile, but it quickly disappears when she looks over at where the paramedics are escorting Daphne downstairs.

"Can I go with her?" Charlie asks one of the police officers.

He gives a hard shake of his head. "I still have to take your statement. She's being admitted to psych, on forty-eight-hour watch. Only family will be allowed to see her."

We've all had enough interaction with the Princeton police to last a lifetime, and I can feel the adrenaline leaving Charlie as she sags against me, telling the officer the night's events. By the time we're done, the ball is back in full swing as if a girl didn't try to kill herself on the roof above.

Jill, Connery, Ava, Tatum, Georgia, and Yates are all waiting for us in the lobby.

The girls rush to Charlie when they see her, wrapping her in a hug.

"Let's get the hell out of here," Prescott says, resting an arm over Ava's shoulder.

I couldn't agree more, and I'm glad that Charlie doesn't fight me. Tatum bows out, wanting to head back to the bar for a final drink. Charlie hugs him goodbye, and when she lets go, they squeeze one another's hands for an extra long beat. Tatum came with Daphne and she left alone. So is he. I feel for the guy, and I can see in his goodbye to Charlotte, that he is saying goodbye to more than the night. It's his goodbye to the girl he loves.

The eight of us, Ava and Prescott, Jill and Connery, Georgia and Yates, and Charlie and me, leave the ball. Outside, we find the night air warm, the wind has died down. The sky is dark, the lamplight leads the way. And looking around, there is a collective exhale. Tonight started on such a high - pampering the girls in luxury. Limo rides and an elaborate ballroom.

Now, none of that matters.

What matters is the real, the tangible. Beating hearts. We're living, breathing. Alive. God, I never want to lose what I have right now.

The stars are out, and we walk along the wide sidewalks, arms draped around our lovers, our friends, our adrenaline still high and none of us quite ready to leave after everything we went through. After everything we saw. We pause at a flight of stairs, and sit, sprawling out. Loosening our ties, the rustling of the gowns the girls wear.

Prescott produces a bottle of champagne. When he pops the cork, we cheer, holding onto the moment. It's not graduation yet, but it feels like the end of an era.

We lean into one another as we pass the bottle, through thick and thin, here we are, with our eyes fixed to the sky. The stars shine brilliantly. Our futures, they do too.

20

CHARLIE

We finally make it back home as the sun begins to rise and reality sets in. My muscles and heart ache with the hard truth of everything that happened.

I sit in the bath that Spencer draws for me, the jets on, meant to relax me. But my body is too tense, and I stare numbly at my fingers. They're raw from gripping onto the ledge, my manicure shot to hell, but I'm alive - and so is Daphne. That's the most important thing. Even though I know she has a hard future ahead of her. Part of me wonders how anyone can ever get over something so devastating, knowing in a way that they're responsible for another person's death.

Spencer gets in the large jacuzzi tub behind me and pulls me back so I'm leaning against his chest. He takes my hand in his gently and studies my fingers. "That looks painful."

"I'm okay." It's more the emotional pain that I'm struggling with now. "I still can't believe Daphne hid that from me all these years. We were roommates when it happened." I shake my head. "To live with that and not have anyone to talk to..."

"She's still at fault, Charlie. She may not have been driving the car, but by not saying anything she's guilty of omission."

"I know." And I do, but I can't help but feel sorry for her, and for the torment she must've been going through, especially after she found out that Shannon had still been alive when they drove away. That one phone call may have saved the girl's life. "What will happen to her?"

"I'm not sure." Spencer runs his knuckles over my shoulder and down my arm. "Her parents have money, so I'm sure they'll get a good lawyer. But it'll mean more press...more media coverage."

"I'm sorry. I know this is hard on you."

He sighs. "I just hope this is the last surprise. Not sure my heart can take anything else."

I twist in his arms. "I know."

His fingers tangle in my damp hair. "I wanted this night to be perfect for you."

"It was. Or at least it was until I was dangling over the side of a building," I tease, but I can tell he doesn't think it's funny.

He grunts. "I can't have anything happen to you, Charlie."

I turn in the tub, facing him. Needing to look in his eyes, needing him to see my heart, in all its ramshackle glory. I've somehow pieced together meaning in all of this. As my fingers slipped from the ledge, as I wondered if I would make it. As life flashed before my eyes, I saw what I needed to see. I know what I need to know.

We're going to be okay.

"You can't protect me from everything, from life. Isn't that the lesson in all of this? We have to keep living, loving, doing our best no matter what. Because Spence, there are no guarantees. Tonight, it was a blindside. We didn't see it coming. But we got through it."

"And if we hadn't?" Spencer asks, his words raw. "If you had fallen... if I had lost you..."

"Then we would have known we had lived each day to its fullest. We wouldn't have regret, we would have memories so beautiful," I tell him, drawing closer to him, my hands on his chiseled jaw. "We would have this love, the love we found."

He kisses me then and I know he understands. Yes, it's messy. Losing Ethan and losing my mom, it was tragic. It was too soon, and their deaths leave us with a missing piece to our hearts.

But also, their lives gave us so much. The time we had, we will never forget it.

"I love you, Charlotte Hayes," he says as he cradles me in his arms. We stand silently from the tub, his arms lifting me up, and he dries me off without a word. He carries me to the bed and my heart is so full that it could burst.

He knows. *He knows me.*

He takes me, softly and slowly. Caressing my skin in a way that sends shivers up and down my spine, sends warmth to my heart. "I love you," I moan as he opens me up, as he enters me. It's soft and tender and exactly what we need.

His fingers lace with mine, pinning me to the bed, my breath shallow, his eyes heavy with need. I feel his pulsing length inside me, hitting me to my core, my deepest place. I moan, gasping for breath.

"Oh god you feel good," he tells me, his mouth

on my ear. I give myself over to him. Every inch of my being, my soul.

We move together in sync, in a rhythm that is better than any playlist we could ever come up with.

The song of our hearts leading the way. Guiding us home.

EPILOGUE I

SPENCER

Two months later...

WE SIT IN CHAIRS, behind the lawn of Nassau Hall as the prestigious Princeton University commencement ceremony begins. The graduation class wears black gowns and caps, and as I sit in the audience, I wait anxiously for Charlotte Hayes' name to be called.

Daniel is at my side, along with Ava and Prescott, and when my girlfriend finally walks across the stage, I stand, clapping. So fucking proud.

She did it. With honors. With pride. With so much integrity it makes me want to be a better man. She fought for this day for most of her life.

Pulling up her bootstraps and making her dreams come true all on her own. Fuck, I wipe my eyes, emotional as she shakes the hand of the president. Everything about this moment is being captured on Prescott's camera and I look at Daniel, his eyes brimming with pride and tears. She did it, our Charlie did it.

And the thing is, it's just the beginning. Charlie is going places and dammit, I'm going there with her.

After the pomp and circumstance, we finally make our way to Charlie. She's posing for a photo with Jill's mother, but when she sees me, she leaps into my arms, smashing the bouquet of roses I have for her.

"You are so fucking amazing," I tell her, spinning her around, her feet off the ground.

Daniel gets her next and he pulls his little girl into a warm embrace. "Your mother would have been so proud, Charlie."

She nods, her eyes glistening with tears. "I know. But I'm so glad you're here, Dad. So glad you're staying for another few weeks."

He laughs. "We'll see how this Michigan boy does in this fancy-schmancy beach town."

"Nantucket isn't fancy," I tell him. "Down to earth, with clam bakes and sand dunes."

"Right," Charlie laughs, jabbing an elbow at my rib. "And multi-million dollar beach properties. Totally chill."

Ava comes over, giving her a hug, and Prescott hands Charlie a bouquet of tulips. "Can't wait for the after party."

"When do you guys head off for Australia?" Charlie asks.

"Not until tomorrow afternoon. Plenty of time to celebrate tonight."

Jill and Connery come over, beaming - and I know Jill is still a little flabbergasted that she is finishing her education at Princeton with a boyfriend. Especially a guy like Connery, old-money and a trust fund as big as mine, though he's never flashy about it.

"So good to see you, sweetheart," Daniel says, giving Jill a hug. "And it's high time I met this boyfriend of yours."

While they are chatting, I wrap my arm around Charlie. "I'm so proud of you."

She looks up at me smiling. "Thanks, Spencer, I couldn't have done it without you."

"Not sure about that," I say, wrapping my arms around her. "You were always going places."

"You guys will be at the party, right?" Connery asks, hustling over. "My parents went all out. They think this is my crowning achievement."

"We wouldn't miss it," Charlie says. "And it's so nice of them to do this for you. For all of us."

"We'll see you there, Connery," I tell him. But I know we won't be there for awhile.

We have a very important stop to make first.

"Why are we downtown?" Charlie asks as we pull into a parking spot. It's a beautiful summer night and the day has been nothing but celebratory. I run my hand over the black box in my suit coat, ready to ask the one question I've been wanting to ask for months.

Now is the time. I didn't want to distract Charlie as she was finishing her coursework, but now she has her degree. *Now* I can ask.

After the commencement, we went for lunch with Daniel, Ava, and Prescott. The fact my parents didn't join us was a hard pill to swallow, but ever since I went public about Ethan's crime, they haven't spoken to me. Bitter is the understatement of the century.

Ava has kept in touch with Mom, but it's stilted. We've gone backwards so many steps. For awhile there, it meant so much to me to have their respect and approval, but now it isn't something I seek, or will ever seek again. It's both relief and heartbreak.

It's sad not celebrating tonight with them. Never in a million years did I think this day would come without them involved. And once it happens, I'll never be able to edit them into this moment.

When I asked Daniel permission to marry his daughter, his eyes grew glassy. He said it made the most sense in the world. That he knew he wasn't losing a daughter, but instead, gaining a son.

Now, we're here. And I'm taking Charlie's hand in mine, leading her to the record store.

"This is random," she says as I push open the door. The owner gives me a nod and dims the lights.

The entire shop is filled with our friends and family. Everyone who was at graduation has returned - for this moment. The one I pray Charlie will never forget.

"My Girl" by The Temptations is blaring

through the sound system, and there are a thousand twinkly lights strung up in the shop.

She turns to me, shaking her head in bewilderment. But it shouldn't be confusing. Falling in love with her was the easiest thing I've ever done.

"What is this?"

I lead her to the center of the shop, amid rows of records, where rose petals cover the floor.

"Spencer?" she gasps.

"Charlie Hayes, I love you. So damn much."

She presses her hands to her heart, and she chokes out, "I love you too."

"I fell in love with you hard and fast, when we're together the world makes more sense. You make me laugh, make me cry, remind me how precious life is. And I want to spend that life with you."

"Oh my god," she whispers as I drop to bended knee and pull out the little black box.

"We both love music and I want the song of our lives to be sung to the same melody."

She smiles as tears run down her cheeks.

"I'm corny," I add, chuckling. "But we both know that. And the thing is, it's the truth, Charlie. I want to marry you and be the rhythm to your blues. The punk to your rock and the R to your B."

Her shoulders shake with laughter, her smile so

wide and our friends, who are standing around us laugh.

I pull back the lid of the box in my hands, revealing an antique five carat emerald cut diamond ring. Looking up at the woman who gives my life meaning in so many ways, I'm more sure of my words than I've ever been in my life. "Marry me Charlie. Be my wife."

She's reaching for me, and I stand. Her lips are on mine before she answers. Her mouth telling me that she wants this as much as I do.

"Yes. I will marry you, Spencer Beckett. All I want is to be yours."

"You are," I tell her, slipping the ring on her finger as everyone claps, cheering. Taking photographs as I pull Charlie into another kiss. The music of The Temptations fills the shop and I kiss my fiancée, with the promise of forever.

EPILOGUE II

CHARLIE

Five Years Later...

Balloons and streamers fall around us, and the crowd of loyal supporters, and friends and family cheer as Spencer's name is announced on the jumbotron behind us.

"Congratulations Congressman." I smile up at my husband, so proud of everything that he's accomplished.

He pulls me close, or at least as close as my protruding belly will allow, and kisses me hard. "I couldn't have done any of this without you."

"I know," I tease, wincing slightly as the baby kicks me hard.

"You okay?" His expression turns serious and he places a hand on my stomach. Cameras flash around us, and I have no doubt the image will be all over the news tomorrow.

Surprisingly, the media ate up our story, loving the whole Cinderella and Prince Charming anecdote. My rags to riches, blue-collar narrative, and Spencer's trust fund with a plan to change the world.

And he will.

Already he's been fundamental in policy changes in healthcare and education, and now as a congressman he'll have even more power to influence change. So, yeah, I'm pretty proud of him. And even more proud of the family we've become.

"It's time for your speech," Jill says approaching us on the dais. She's been his campaign manager for two years now, and we both know he wouldn't be standing here tonight without her.

I'm not sure how she juggles everything. Connery asked her to marry him a few months after graduation, and they had their first child ten months later. They have two little boys now, and another one on the way. But it hasn't slowed her down a bit.

Another pain has a small cold sweat breaking

out across my forehead, but I hide it the best I can. Squeezing Spencer's hand, I kiss his cheek and nod for him to take the microphone. As he starts into his speech, I make my way off the stage.

Ava and Prescott are both waiting behind the stage, and my sister-in-law wraps her arms around me. "This is so huge. I just wish..." Tears fill her eyes and she blinks them away.

"I know," I say, not needing her to say the words. She wishes her parents were here, and even though Spencer hasn't said anything, I know he feels the same.

But Geoffrey passed away three years ago of a massive coronary embolism, and Suzanne hasn't been the same since. She spends most of her time in Palm Springs, no longer doing the charity work that used to fill her time.

The Beckett foundation is in my care now. It wasn't something I sought out. Actually I'd fought Spencer on it when he offered it to me. Running a multi-million dollar foundation was never something I'd considered. But after I graduated with my master's degree and getting to know the foundation, I knew it was what I had to do, because the potential was so much more than what Suzanne had done with it.

Another pain makes my stomach tighten, and I squeeze Ava's hand.

"What's wrong?" Ava asks, frowning.

"Nothing." I grit my teeth until the pain subsides. "I think the baby is celebrating with us."

Ava rubs my stomach and smiles. "I can't wait to meet my niece."

Prescott chuckles, an arm resting over her shoulder. "Next you'll be wanting one of your own."

Ava smiles up at him, her eyes shining with love and adoration. "You're the one who's been talking about it."

"Really?" I ask. Sometimes Prescott surprises me. He still has his moments of assholeness, but he's been good to Ava. They got married last summer on the beach in front of our Nantucket home. The same place Spencer and I said our vows four years ago.

Prescott winks. "Can't have Spencer outdoing me."

I roll my eyes and laugh as Georgia and Yates approach.

"Spencer is killing it out there," Yates says as a cheer rings out from the crowd.

"Of course he is," Prescott adds.

Yates smacks his back. "You're not doing too

bad yourself. It's nothing to scoff at being a member of the U.S. House of Representatives at twenty-eight."

Prescott just shrugs, and I know he has ambition for more. With Ava at his side, he just might get it.

My phone buzzes and I smile when I see Tatum's number on the screen. I excuse myself from the group and take the call.

"Hey," I say, finding a couch to sit down on.

"Shit, sorry," he says. "I didn't think you'd pick up. I was just going to leave a message congratulating Spencer on his big win."

"You're not interrupting. I was actually looking for an excuse to find a quiet place and sit down."

"You're due soon, right?"

"Any day." I rub my belly. "How are you doing?"

"I'm good."

"That's not much of an answer." I take off one of my heels and rub my foot, which is slightly swollen and aching.

He sighs. "Not much to really tell."

"Come on, you're a big-time NFL star now, I'm sure you've got some stories. Are you seeing anyone?"

"Nah. Every chick I meet only wants me for my wallet or my..." He coughs.

"Oh, must be hard having all those girls throwing themselves at you," I tease.

He grunts and changes the subject. "So, did you and Charming pick out a name yet?"

"Yes, but we're keeping it a secret until she's born. And I expect you to come see her."

"You know I'll be there."

"Good. Because we want you to be her godfather."

"Don't you have to be religious or something?" he asks, but I hear the emotion in his voice.

I laugh. "You're as religious as we are."

"Yeah. I guess that's true." There's a short moment of silence before he says, "I got a call from Daphne a few days ago."

"How is she?" I feel terrible that we haven't kept in touch, but after the incident at the ball, she refused to see me. She wrote me a letter a few years back, apologizing, saying she was embarrassed about what she'd done and she hoped that I'd forgive her, but I hadn't heard from her again.

"She's married now. Said she's happy. I think she was just trying to get some game tickets from me." He chuckles.

"Sounds like her."

"Speaking of crazy," Tatum says. "I saw Winslow in the news. Shit, I can't believe she married that old dude, he could be her grandfather."

I laugh. "You always did tell it like it is." Winslow got what she always wanted, a rich, political husband. "It was good hearing from you, Tatum. Come by the house soon. Okay?"

After I hang up, I close my eyes, listening to the low hum of people talking outside. Spencer must be finished his speech. But I stay here for a few more minutes, breathing through another Braxton Hicks.

"There you are." Spencer comes into the room, undoing his tie and the top button of his shirt, he crouches in front of me and takes my foot, starting to massage it. "We should get you home."

"I'm okay. I just needed a couple minutes to rest."

He holds my shoe in one hand and smirks. "Looks like my Cinderella lost her shoe again."

"You're so corny."

He chuckles and places the shoe on my foot. "Yeah, but you love it."

"I love you, Mr. Congressman."

"I like the sound of that."

The baby is moving like crazy and I press Spencer's hand to my belly. "Feel that?"

"She's dancing up a storm."

"I guess," I say, grimacing as another Braxton Hicks tightens my belly. "But it's more than that. It's like she's getting ready for something." I exhale slowly as Spencer massages my neck.

"Her due date is in two weeks, it makes sense she's preparing for her entrance."

Before I can say anything, there is a pop. And it's not the sound of a champagne cork celebrating Spencer's victory.

It's my water. Breaking. Thank God we aren't still up on stage. "Oh my god."

"Charlie," Spencer, says, his expression a mix of excitement and fear. "She's coming today."

"We never seem to celebrate one thing at a time, do we?" I ask, remembering how he proposed at graduation five years ago. "I don't want this to ruin your big night," I say, thinking about the auditorium of people here celebrating his win.

"I love you Charlie Beckett, but that is the most ridiculous thing you've ever said," he laughs. "Now let me call an ambulance, there is no way in hell I'm letting you get in a car without a medical professional."

Jill comes in looking for Spencer, and her mouth drops when she sees the puddle of water on the floor. "Oh my gosh, it's happening!" She immediately starts barking orders into her headset and I try to concentrate as a contraction moves through me. Okay, apparently I've been having real ones all afternoon, not fake ones.

"You're going to do great Charlie," Jill says. "You just focus on that baby. We'll take care of everything else."

Every mother says labor is hard and none of them are exaggerating. And only one hour after my water breaks, I'm begging the doctor to give me drugs, but she insists it's too late.

"You're almost there, Charlotte, the baby is crowning," my doctor tells me.

"Already?" I ask, my body betraying me as another contraction has me screaming for mercy.

"I can see her head, Charlie. Only a few more pushes," she says.

"Can you see her, Spence?" I ask, shaking. "Can you see our baby?"

His eyes are so bright with love and devotion as he looks at me. "She's got a lot of hair."

"Really?" I ask as another contraction rips through me. Tears stream down my face and I think I might be breaking Spencer's fingers, but I don't care. I don't care about anything besides holding a healthy baby in my arms.

A new song comes onto the speakers and I instantly start crying all over again. Spencer created the most perfect labor playlist, but this one is "Here Comes the Sun." The song that I consider to be *ours*. He played it for me on the worst day of my life, the day of Mom's funeral. But it's a song with hope, and that's what I need right now. Because I don't think I can get through this labor without it.

"Your dad's here," Ava says, entering the hospital room. "Can he come in?"

I nod, maybe some women are more modest, but if my dad wants to be here when his granddaughter enters the world, I won't keep him away.

He comes in and kisses my forehead. "Oh Charlie, you're doing so good," he says. "So good."

"I can't do it," I moan. "It hurts."

"You got this," Ava says. "You do, sweetie." She is the best sister-in-law in the world and when she tells me I got this, I believe her. "Besides, you need to go fast. Prescott has a pool going in the waiting room on when you'll deliver and if you do this in the next twenty minutes he loses."

"And who wins?" Spencer asks, running a damp rag over my forehead.

"Me," the doctor says with a smile.

The conversation helps me relax for a moment, regain my strength, and when the next contraction comes, I push.

And then she is here. Not just like that of course, but fast enough for me to get through it without falling apart. She is a writhing naked mess of a perfect human and she is mine. Spencer and I made her and when the doctor places our baby to my chest, I weep. Tears of love and hope and joy. Tears filled with memories of my past and visions of her future and dreams for this life we get to navigate together.

Spencer is kissing me and kissing her. The room seems to swirl around us for a moment. The doctor and nurses and family disappear and all I see is my daughter and her father.

"You did it," he says.

"We did it," I say as he kisses me.

"I'm so proud to be your husband," he tells me,

our foreheads touching, our sweet little one so tiny and soft and perfect.

We are brought back to the room as my dad cheers in a way only a proud grandpa from Michigan can do. "She's perfect," Dad says. "You did so good, kid," he tells me, getting choked up. The fact that he is here means more than he will ever know.

"Hello, Heather," I say, having chosen her name after my mother. I look into my daughter's eyes. "I'm your mommy."

"She needs a tiara," Spencer says softly. "Our little princess."

"I hope she has a fairy tale ending just like us," I say, looking into Spencer's eyes.

He kisses me again, so many emotions swirling in his blue eyes. "We're not even close to the ending, sweetheart."

Epilogue Three
Three years later...
Spencer

"Mo, Mo, Daddy." Heather claps her chubby

toddler hands, demanding I read her another story. She grabs a book "Sis one, pease, Daddy."

I'm wrapped around her finger, and she knows it. How could I not be? She has the same hazel eyes as her mother, same pouty lips. She's as feisty as her mother is too. She dances around the house in her tutu, belting out songs from her favorite cartoons, and when she sings "One Day My Prince Will Come," Charlie and I melt. Every. Single. Time.

Heather knows this too and uses it to her advantage.

As she should.

"One more, and then bed, alright Princess?"

"I want 'Rella," she says, reaching for her well-worn storybook. "Pease, Daddy?"

I open up the book and read her the adapted fairy tale of Cinderella. By the time I'm a few pages in, her eyes are closed and she's sleeping soundly. I close the book and place it on her bedside table, turning off the light. I kiss her nose, her cheeks, her forehead.

I thought I knew what love was when I met Charlie. Turns out having a baby girl expands a man's heart all over again.

I close her door, leaving it slightly ajar, and find Charlie downstairs in the kitchen. She's pouring hot water into a mug for tea. I know she's had a long few days. Work has kept me out of town as I've been working on new legislation for policy reform for how we take care of our homeless population. And Charlie has been fundraising tirelessly for a new community center and shelter, which will also house a health care clinic and offer job training.

Her passion for her community is remarkable, and she was recently listed in the Washington D.C.'s Thirty Under Thirty List - which is pretty incredible in a district like this where accomplished people are everywhere you turn.

Charlie though, is giving them all a run for their money. God, I love her.

I wrap my arms around her, kissing her neck.

She laughs, setting down the kettle. Then she spins around in my arms. "Did she go down okay?"

I run my hands over my wife's rounding tummy. "She's out cold."

Charlie bites her lip. "It's a shame this tea will get cold." She lifts an eyebrow.

I pull her closer, my hand cupping her full tits. "Oh yeah? Why's that?" I ask, squeezing her perfect ass.

"Because your wife is experiencing second

trimester..." She licks her lips and smiles. "Cravings."

"I'm here to serve." I kiss her, hard. "Your wish is my command."

"Well, I *wish* that you would have your way with me," she says smiling, running her hand over my slacks, my cock hard as she touches me. God, I need her.

"You get me so fucking hard, Charlie," I groan.

She giggles. "Good. That will serve me well."

Moments later we're in our room, the door closed, and I'm stripping my wife from her sweater and leggings, her panties and bra. God, she's so fucking perfect. She tugs on my tie, unbuttoning my dress shirt, running her hands over my chest. "You've been working out on the road, haven't you?"

"You like that?" I ask as she unbuckles my pants, running my hands over her tight nipples. She looks so hot pregnant. When she suggested we try again for another baby, I was more than pleased. She looks so fucking hot knocked up - her tits huge, her skin glowing, her body growing our child. Fuck, it's hot as hell.

I take her to bed, my cock hard and thick as she strokes my length. "I missed you," I tell her. It's been two days, but it's two days too long. "Next time you're coming with me."

She smiles, her head on the pillow, her hair longer now and spilling over the sheets. She looks like a goddess. My goddess. "I won't argue with that."

I run my hand over her pussy, she's wet and I look down at her with need. "You weren't lying when you told me you had some cravings."

She whimpers as I touch her, and my fingers circle her clit, her back arching as she revels in the pleasure.

"I need you in me," she whispers. "Now."

I enter her, running my hands over her skin, my fingers threading through her hair. God, she smells good, like home. She whimpers beneath me, and I revel in the moment, having her in my arms. Our bodies connect, the way our heart and souls already have. I was her first and she is my forever.

"I love you, Spencer," she breathes against me as we both finish, our bodies pulsing and hot and so fucking complete I could cry. God, I love this woman.

After, I cradle her, my hands on her round belly. "I can't believe we're having a boy," she says as I kiss her bare skin.

"Our little prince." I cup her cheek, longing, always longing to have her in my arms. Just like this.

"We found our happily ever after, didn't we?" she asks sleepily, her eyes closing and I kiss her softly.

She's right, except our fairy tale wasn't written in a storybook. This love, it was written in our hearts.

C.M. SEABROOK

Amazon bestselling author C.M. Seabrook writes hot, steamy romances with possessive bad boys, and the passionate, fiery women who love them. Swoon-worthy romances from the heart!

For something a little different, read Chantel Seabrook's Shifter, Reverse Harem, and Fantasy books here https://amzn.to/2MTiItI

SIGN UP FOR C.M. Seabrook's NEWSLETTER FOR LATEST NEWS!
   http://eepurl.com/cB56an

ALSO BY C.M. SEABROOK

Men with Wood Series

Second Draft

Second Shot

Fighting Blind Series

Theo

Moody

Wild Irish Series

Wild Irish

Tempting Irish

Taming Irish

Savages & Saints Series

Torment

Gravity

Salvage

Beast

Standalones

Melting Steel

FRANKIE LOVE

Frankie Love writes sexy stories about bad boys and mountain men. As a thirty-something mom who is ridiculously in love with her own bearded hottie, she believes in love-at-first-sight and happily-ever-afters. She also believes in the power of a quickie.

>Find Frankie here:
>*www.frankielove.net*
>*frankieloveromance@gmail.com*

>*JOIN FRANKIE LOVE'S MAILING LIST*

>*AND NEVER MISS A RELEASE!*

ALSO BY FRANKIE LOVE

The Mountain Man's Babies

TIMBER

BUCKED

WILDER

HONORED

CHERISHED

BUILT

CHISELED

HOMEWARD

SIX MEN OF ALASKA

The Wife Lottery

The Wife Protectors

The Wife Gamble

The Wife Code

The Wife Pact

The Wife Legacy

MOUNTAIN MEN OF LINESWORTH

MOUNTAIN MAN CANDY

MOUNTAIN MAN CAKE

MOUNTAIN MAN BUN

#OBSESSED

MOUNTAIN MEN OF BEAR VALLEY

Untamed Virgins

Untamed Lovers

Untamed Daddy

Untamed Fiance

Stand-Alone Romance

B.I.L.F.

BEAUTY AND THE MOUNTAIN MAN

HIS Everything

HIS BILLION DOLLAR SECRET BABY

UNTAMED

RUGGED

HIS MAKE BELIEVE BRIDE

HIS KINKY VIRGIN

WILD AND TRUE

BIG BAD WOLF

MISTLETOE MOUNTAIN: A MOUNTAIN MAN'S CHRISTMAS

Our Virgin

Protecting Our Virgin

Craving Our Virgin

Forever Our Virgin

F*ck Club

A-List F*ck Club

Small Town F*ck Club

Modern-Mail Order Brides

CLAIMED BY THE MOUNTAIN MAN

ORDERED BY THE MOUNTAIN MAN

WIFED BY THE MOUNTAIN MAN

EXPLORED BY THE MOUNTAIN MAN

CROWN ME

COURTED BY THE MOUNTAIN PRINCE

CHARMED BY THE MOUNTAIN PRINCE

CROWNED BY THE MOUNTAIN PRINCE

CROWN ME, PRINCE: The Complete Collection

Las Vegas Bad Boys

ACE

KING

MCQUEEN

JACK

Los Angeles Bad Boys

COLD HARD CASH

HOLLYWOOD HOLDEN

SAINT JUDE

THE COMPLETE COLLECTION

Made in the USA
Middletown, DE
06 February 2019